Romancing the Flower Shop Girl

A Romantic Comedy Novel

ANGIE PEPPER

Chapter 1

Tina Gardenia was on the verge of crying. A bundle of blue roses sat before her on the prep counter. They were so tacky, so unnatural. Natural roses came in so many wonderful colors, but people preferred the white ones tinted with blue dye. People didn't always have the best taste. Florists were supposed to help, but the customer was always right. Even if they wanted dyed blue roses.

She picked up one rose, cupping the blossom in her palm as she stripped the thorns off with a knife.

Her eyes felt hot and itchy. They hadn't recovered from the previous night's sad movie, which should have come with an Ugly Cry warning. It served her right for picking one with a dog on the picture. She should have known the dog would die. Now her tear ducts were probably permanently damaged. She blinked hard, but it didn't help.

The door chime let out a chirp. Someone walked into Gardenia Flowers. By the sound of his steps, it was a man, and not a small one.

Tina's gaze went first to the boots. They were motorcycle boots. And they were big.

Next, her gaze climbed up his jeans. And what a climb it was, over long legs clad in denim, and noticeably muscled thighs. Her mouth went dry, and she nearly looked away out of modesty but didn't. She was having a good day, and on good days she didn't feel like a shrinking violet at all.

The man wore a black shirt with a bike logo, stretched tight across his chest muscles. He was so big, and the flower shop was so tiny, that he had to turn his body sideways to squeeze past the ferns. His presence in the cramped shop reminded Tina of that old expression: Bull in a china shop.

Tina watched him with detached amusement, the way she watched comedy movies. The man was in his early thirties, which would have made him a potential dating prospect, if it weren't for those big boots and that tall, manly frame. The guy fighting his way through the fern jungle wasn't her type at all. She usually went for skinny video game or movie geeks. Guys who were more boys than men. The sort of guys who didn't have their lives figured out, either, and therefore didn't bug her to "get out of her comfort zone." Tina liked her comfort zone. It was called that for a reason.

The man had breached the fern jungle and was now looking over the other tropical houseplants as he made his way toward the counter.

Tina's heart started to pound. This was no comedy movie. This was real life, and it was happening in real time.

The closer he got, the more easily she could see the definition in his arms, his shoulders, even his neck. Whenever she saw a bunch of muscles, she got stupid and giggly on the inside. One time, she'd tried to buy some men's underwear as a Christmas present for someone, but she'd left the store empty-handed because the hunky beefcakes on the packaging made her feel funny. She wasn't nearly as squeamish as her best friend, but Tina had her moments.

This guy was fully clothed, thankfully. He had about a week's worth of beard. It was light brown, like his wavy hair. His face had strong, balanced proportions. He looked like the kind of guy who didn't need a bottle opener. He'd use those big fists of his, or his teeth.

Despite the bike-logo T-shirt, the large man in Tina's tiny flower shop wasn't intimidating in a biker gang sort of way. He was artfully scruffy, like a famous athlete on his day off. Was he an athlete? There were a few famous hockey players that lived in the neighborhood. This guy would be a menace to the other team, especially raised up even taller on a pair of skates.

Suddenly, things clicked into place for Tina. The biker boots, the black T-shirt, and the rugged good looks. She'd heard about this guy. He'd been the talk of the neighborhood for weeks. Everyone was agitated about him. That morning at Delilah's, Maggie had barely been able to pour Tina her usual tea, she'd been so upset about him.

The man sniffing a bouquet of scentless irises had to be him.

Luca Lowell.

He finally reached the flower shop's counter.

Rather than ask him if he needed help, Tina held her breath. She'd been about to say something friendly, but then he'd smiled and looked her right in the eyes. His attention on her had felt like headlights washing over a frozen deer.

The man had the most beautiful blue eyes she'd ever seen. Or possibly the most beautiful blue eyes in existence, period. Everyone in the neighborhood had been talking about him, but nobody had mentioned his eyes. How could a person leave out a detail like that?

The man cleared his throat and said, "I see I've caught you at a bad time." His voice was deep, yet surprisingly gentle, given his scruffy appearance.

His relaxed approach had allowed her to catch her breath, so she answered quickly, "This isn't a bad time." She picked up another rose and whipped the knife through the thorns. "I'm just stripping."

The sunlight coming in the front window caught in the corners of his breathtaking eyes and sparkled. "You're not stripping," he said matter-of-factly.

"Honestly, I am," she said.

He stood on his toes and looked over the counter, peering all the way down to her feet.

She felt the heat of his gaze as he took a visual tour. First at her tennis shoes, then up her bare legs to her jean shorts, which weren't even shorts, but an old pair of jeans that she'd hacked off below the knees. He raised his eyebrows and continued his sightseeing journey, up over her greenery-stained, three-sizes-too-large sweatshirt. The young florist's *spectacular* ensemble was topped off by a fashion-throwback pink scrunchie that held her curly brown hair high on her head. The scrunchie was actually a big improvement over the blue elastics she usually used—the kind of utilitarian band that came around the base of sturdy greenery. But he couldn't have known that. All he must have seen, Tina feared, was a sloppy girl with dark circles under her eyes from crying all week like a loser.

He finished the visual tour, rocked back on his heels, and said, "If you think this is stripping, you're doing it all wrong."

"Oh, but I am stripping," she said, slowing down to a standstill so she didn't stab herself with the knife by accident. "Stripping thorns."

"Ah," he said, tipping his head back in a friendly way. "The less-popular but still completely valid form of stripping. My mistake."

He leaned over the counter, resting his elbow the way someone did if they were planning to stick around a while. He reached out with one big paw of a hand.

"I'm Luca Lowell," he said. "I bought that dirty old run-down garage down the street."

She knew that. Everyone on the block knew that. They'd been talking about Luca Lowell ever since he'd taken over the local garage, which had been dirty, and had been run-down, but had also been well-loved by many, including Tina.

She set down the blue rose and the knife and shook his hand. Her small palm disappeared in his warm embrace. She hoped he didn't notice how sweaty hers was. He had calluses. So did she. And yet their hands fit together perfectly.

"I'm Tina Gardenia, like the sign on the door," she said. "And I've heard all about you, Luca Lowell. Folks around here are not very happy with you."

"They're not?" He raised an eyebrow. "What folks?"

"Everyone. The whole neighborhood has been getting their cars serviced at Ralph's for generations. Now what are they going to do?"

"They'll have to trade their cars in and get something better. Bikes."

She laughed then stopped abruptly. "You're serious!"

"I am. The garage isn't being shut down permanently. It's just changing focus. Once we reopen, we'll specialize in servicing all kinds of bikes. This is the best location in the whole city for a business like mine. All the local hotshot athletes have been looking for a place they can trust." His blue eyes broke away from hers to take in more of the flower shop. It was small, and there wasn't much to take in. "And scooters, too," he said. "Do you have a scooter, Tina? You look like the scooter type."

She liked the sound of her name on his lips.

"A scooter? I'll think about it."

It was the truth. She'd never considered owning a scooter, but Luca Lowell made it sound fun. Maybe Tina Gardenia *was* a scooter kind of girl. In high school, she'd been on the wrestling team. She wasn't afraid to get physical, and her core was strong from lifting heavy buckets of water.

"Tina, I have a question for you." He rested his big knuckles on the counter between them and gave her an earnest look. "What do you know about women?"

"I know a few things about women. Plus I actually am one, despite current appearances."

"Do you mean the big sweatshirt? I saw right through your disguise."

"What do you need to know about women?"

"I need to know how to not make them mad at me. Or, since that's not too likely, how to get them to forgive me when I do inevitably make them mad."

Tina's heart sank. Luca Lowell was not her type at all, and yet knowing he already had a girlfriend was ruining her previously good day.

"So that's why you're here," she said, nodding. "You need flowers to apologize with."

"Does that actually work?"

"We wouldn't still be in business if it didn't."

He scoffed. "I can't believe women are so easy."

She scoffed back. "If they really were that easy, men like you wouldn't come to places like this."

He held up both hands. "I didn't mean to ruffle your feathers."

"I don't ruffle that easy." She waved a hand. "So, about this woman who's mad at you. Exactly what did you do?"

He smirked. "Nothing I won't do again."

Classic bad boy. And this was exactly why Tina didn't date guys like Luca.

She asked, "Have you considered… not doing that thing anymore?"

"Where's the fun in that? Maybe it's one of my favorite things." He grinned, dazzling her with great-looking teeth.

"So, you need an apology arrangement?"

"That depends. Do you offer a money-back guarantee?"

"No, but if she kills you, we'll do your funeral for half price." She chuckled at her own joke. "Florist humor."

He kept smiling but didn't laugh.

He asked, "Can I get something by closing tonight?"

"Absolutely. Do you have a budget? Is there a type of flower that holds a special meaning for the two of you?"

"Surprise me." He dropped some cash on the counter. "Is this enough?"

Her eyes widened at the sight of the cash. The bike garage business must have been profitable. She also happened to notice he didn't wear a wedding band. That meant the woman who was mad at him probably wasn't a wife. That shouldn't have cheered her up, since he wasn't her type, but it did.

"That's more than enough," she said, then she went on to crack another joke she'd made countless times over the years working there. "The flowers should work, but if she doesn't take you back, you can always marry me. I'll throw in my sister, too."

He took a step back. "What?"

She pointed her thumb behind her, toward the door to the office. "That joke makes more sense if my sister's actually here."

"I'm sure it does," he said.

The door chimed with another customer coming in.

Luca gave the young florist in the sloppy clothes a long, appraising look, tinged with curiosity. Then he turned and walked back out again in those big motorcycle boots.

She stared at the door for several minutes. The scent of his masculine cologne lingered in the air. Or maybe it was just the flowers all around, plus her imagination. Either way, it was pleasant.

Tina's customer service reflexes finally kicked in, and she offered the new customer help. The customer replied that she was just looking for now.

Tina picked up Luca's money and smelled it. She expected the stack of bills to smell like Luca, but it just smelled like the inside of a pocket. A freshly laundered pocket, at least. Tina couldn't say the same for her tattered cut-off shorts.

The customer saw Tina sniffing the money, gave her a funny look, and then left without buying anything.

Tina Gardenia sighed and stared at the front door.

Luca Lowell was every bit as handsome as folks in the neighborhood had been telling her, even if they had left out the detail about his dazzling blue eyes. Time was marching on, and things were changing, despite everyone's wishes to keep everything the same. Luca Lowell would be working right down the street from her, day in and day out, for years. Maybe even forever. Businesses that made it past five years in the neighborhood tended to sprout deep roots and stick around forever.

The first thing Tina needed to do after making Luca's flower arrangement was... look into purchasing a scooter.

Obviously.

Chapter 2

It took Tina Gardenia of Gardenia Flowers a whopping three hours to create Luca Lowell's apology bouquet.

She'd started off by making it ugly. Extremely ugly. Pink carnations. Baby's breath. All the wilted stuff waiting to be composted. Tina thought that if an ugly bouquet could push this already-angry woman over the top, the woman would have to break up with Luca.

And then what?

Luca and Tina would just be friends at first, on account of his recent breakup. Their friendship would become intimate, but not physical. Not at first. Then, one day, he'd walk into the flower shop, lock the front door, and take her in his arms. He'd knock all the paperwork off the desk in the office and demand to have her immediately. Like in the movies.

She shivered at the thought of Luca Lowell touching her with those big hands of his. He was a real man. Tina's boyfriends had been just that. Boys. Whenever they'd tried to take charge and dominate, it always made her laugh. How could you take a guy seriously when he got up early on a Saturday morning to play video games?

One time, she'd been on a blind date with a guy who'd pulled out his phone, mid-conversation, to bid on something on Ebay. Was it a sensible item going for a reasonable price? No. It was an auction for virtual spaceship weapons. He'd won the auction but lost the chance at a second date. Tina liked geeks, but they couldn't be *too* geeky. Paying real money for imaginary stuff was too far.

That date had been over a year ago. Maybe she shouldn't have been so picky, because she hadn't had a date since. In hindsight, Mr. Spaceship Weapons didn't seem so bad when she was home alone on a Saturday night.

Tina finished the bouquet. She'd discarded the ugly parts—which had been ninety percent of it—and remade the whole thing with their best flowers. The arrangement was dripping with orchids, but in a tasteful way. Sort of. The secret to a gorgeous arrangement was to go a little too far, which Tina had.

She tidied up her workstation and admired her work. It turned out her pride as a florist was stronger than her desire to sabotage Luca's relationship. The arrangement was stunning.

Luca came back in at closing.

He had flecks of paint all over him, most likely from his renovations at the garage. Everything from the tip of his strong nose to the tips of his wide fingers was spotted in paint. He reminded her of a cupcake covered in sprinkles. A very handsome cupcake.

"All done," she said with a professional air. "If this isn't to your liking, I'd be happy to make some substitutions." She didn't *actually* want to take it apart, but if he stood there and chatted with her while she did it, that wouldn't have been so bad.

"Those flowers are almost as pretty as you," he said.

She pretended to gag. "Gee, thanks, mister. I've never heard that one before." She'd only heard it at least once a day, her whole working life.

"How's your handwriting?"

"It's legible," she said. "You say the words, and I'll write 'em." She grabbed a pen and a note card.

"Just put down the usual."

"The usual? You want me to write 'Sorry I'm such a jerk' on here?"

He chuckled. "If that's the usual, then I guess it'll do."

"It's your funeral," she said, then wrote the note: *Sorry I'm such a jerk.*

Immediately, she changed her mind and ripped up the card. The Florist Code must have kicked in. Florists were like doctors in that they pledged, unofficially, anyway, to first do no harm.

"Why'd you rip that up?" he asked.

She braced herself as she looked up into his breathtaking blue eyes. Holding on to the edge of the counter would keep her from falling in.

"Luca, you asked me what I know about women. Let me give you a bit of advice. There's not a woman out there who wants to get *the usual.*"

"You don't know the particular woman I'm dealing with."

"Apparently, I don't." She held out the pen. "Write the note yourself."

He took the pen from her hand. His fingers grazed her fingers in three separate and distinct spots. She felt the contact in every part of her body.

He picked up a fresh card from the stack on the counter.

In simple block letters, he wrote: SORRY I'M A JERK. -LUCA

He looked up at her, a devilish grin on his lips. "Hope you don't mind me plagiarizing you."

She shrugged. "Good luck with that," she said.

He leaned across the counter. For a panicked moment, she imagined he was coming in to kiss her. He was so close. His wavy brown hair brushed her cheek, then he pulled away.

He hadn't been coming in for a kiss after all. Tina had made the bouquet in one of the largest of the vases they carried. Luca was a big guy, but he'd had to carefully wrap his arms around the big arrangement. He held it to his chest, the highest orchids touching his nose. He blew them away, and they smacked him right back.

"These flowers are fresh," he said. "I couldn't have given you enough cash for all this. I may not know a tulip from a daffodil, but these don't look cheap. Can I give you some more money? Take it from me. I insist. My wallet's in my back pocket."

Tina chewed her lower lip and considered doing it. Not for the money. Only for the back pocket. Her sister would have done it without hesitation. But Tina was not her sister, so she politely declined.

"What you gave me worked out perfectly," she said. "If anything, I owe you change."

"Keep the change," he said. "Everyone loves change."

He thanked her then fought his way through the ferns again to reach the front door. "I swear this jungle is thicker now," he muttered.

Tina made a mental note to rearrange the ferns to make it easier for men like Luca to find their way to her.

When he got to the door, Luca said, "I can see why everyone in the 'hood has such high praise for this store."

"Thanks. You can leave a review online, if you'd like. It helps us a lot."

A slow smile spread across his face. "I could, but I prefer to keep things more personal."

Just then, the door opened. Tina's sister, the one she'd joked about throwing in as a two-for-one-brides deal, and also the one who would have happily dug into all of Luca's pockets just for giggles, was coming in.

"Hello," Megan said to Luca.

He nodded. "Hello and goodbye." He left without another word.

Tina's sister walked up to the counter, her eyes and mouth wide open. "Who was that big hunk of man-candy with half the store's flowers?"

"Some lucky girl's boyfriend."

"Ugh. Hate on me all you want for being a cliché, but it's true that the best ones are always taken. Or geeks. Or live with their mother."

Tina shook her head. "Meenie, *we* live with our mother."

Megan, whom Tina usually called Meenie, shrugged. "So? It's not a bad thing for girls to live with their mom."

Tina started closing the cash register and running the end of day reports.

Megan came to look over her shoulder then wrapped her arms around her sister and gave her a hug. "Rough day?"

Tina shrugged off the unwanted hug. "No. What are you doing? Did you stick something on my back?"

"Would I do something like that to my favorite sister?"

"You'd do that to your only sister."

Megan came in for another hug, which was really a cross between a regular person's hug and a wrestling hold. Both sisters had been on the wrestling team in high school. With Megan, nobody had been surprised. Tina's interest in wrestling surprised people, but it wasn't really anyone's business what she did to let off steam.

As Megan squeezed her sister, she said, "Tina, I saw the blue roses in the cooler. Don't act like everything's fine when I know it isn't. Prom's coming up soon, and then…"

She didn't have to say it. The sisters had been through ten years of Tina falling apart at prom season, especially if anyone ordered blue roses.

"I'm fine," Tina said, wriggling her way out of the wrestling hold and reversing it.

Megan squawked in protest and sputtered, "Stop strangling me, you psycho."

Tina released the hold. "You started it."

A red-faced Megan put her hands on her hips and stared at her sister. "If you keep doing everything the same way, nothing's ever going to change."

Tina turned back to the cash register and the printouts. "Stop looking at me like that. I'm not going to your loser support group."

Megan snorted. "As if they'd even want you in the group."

"I don't need talk therapy. I'm fine."

"If you really *were* fine, you might do more than work here, hang out with Rory, and hide away with your sad movies. What was going on last night? I had my window open and I heard some horrible sounds coming from the cottage. Were you torturing a wild creature in there? I haven't heard sounds like that since we gave Muffins his anti-dandruff bath."

"It was just a stupid movie with a golden retriever. I should know better. The dog on the poster always dies. People who make movies with dogs are the worst."

"But it's not just the movie. Admit it. You always get bad this time of year."

Tina had never, ever admitted it to anyone but herself, and she wasn't about to start. If you ever showed people your vulnerable side, sooner or later they would use it against you.

Tina cursed and slammed the cash drawer shut.

"Leave me alone," Tina said. "If you don't like what you hear, keep your window shut. And stop spying on me."

"Leave you alone?" Megan narrowed her eyes. "Careful what you wish for, because one of these days, you might get exactly what you ask for."

Tina rolled her eyes and walked away. Megan meant well, but she was a sister, and nobody could get on someone's nerves like a sister.

Megan yelled out, "Hey! What's going on with the till? Did you do a cash drop?"

"Not yet."

"Well? Where are you going? Are you actually walking away from me?"

Tina called over her shoulder, "Since you like getting involved so much, you can close up the shop yourself."

Chapter 3

When Tina got home, the lights inside her place were on. That meant her best friend, Rory Taylor, would be waiting for her inside. Rory wouldn't take a key for herself—too intimate—but she did regularly use a hidden key to let herself into the place the Gardenia family called *the cottage*. It was actually a converted former garage, and it sat in her mother's backyard. Tina and Megan did live with their mother, but at least Tina had a bit of yard as a moat between her and the other two.

The cottage had been featured on a TV show about tiny home living. The siding was corrugated metal, painted an indigo blue. The windows were salvaged and mismatched, but all painted the same shade of red. Every window had its own exterior flower box, and every flower box was filled with colorful blossoms. How could a person possibly be more comfortable than that?

The cottage wasn't the only tiny home on the street. For years, homeowners in the neighborhood had been taking advantage of the city's new zoning. Some people built brand-new mini-houses to rent out, and others, like Tina's mother, converted their garages.

At first, everybody had complained about the construction, the extra cars parked on the street, the destruction of the neighborhood. City Hall's push for higher density was the End of Days.

But then the most vocal complainers start building mini-houses in their own backyards, and the ruckus died down.

Tina entered the cottage and found Rory seated at the big—relative to the size of the home—desktop computer. Tina had bought the computer secondhand from an old boyfriend because she'd planned to teach herself graphic design, or programming, or something. So far, she'd only used it to look at takeout menus and social media.

"Hey, gorgeous," Tina said. "Are you here for that booty call?" She knew it would annoy Rory to be greeted that way because it included the phrase *booty call*.

Rory jumped up and shook her whole body, like a dog stepping out of the ocean, to communicate her disgust.

To call Rory Taylor quirky would have been an understatement. She was unlike anyone else Tina knew. Rory was, and had always been, mortified by any mention of sex, in conversation, or in books or movies. A single word, such as *moist*, could send her screaming from the room.

Rory and Tina had been best friends since they'd met in kindergarten. Tina loved Rory as much as—or even more than—her sister. Rory was often mistaken for one of the Gardenia girls. With her curly brown hair, she fit right in with her family. She was in most of the annual family photos.

When the girls had been teens, Rory spent more time at the Gardenia house than at hers. Things were rough at Rory's house. The more you knew about Rory, the more it explained her quirks.

Tina tried to be sensitive to her best friend's issues, but that didn't mean teasing was off the table. If Tina was ever losing an argument with Rory, Tina would drop one of Rory's no-no words into the conversation, and Rory would clam right up.

"You're home early," Rory said. "Did you sell out of flowers?"

"Ha ha," Tina said. "I got Meenie to close up the shop."

"But it's her day off." Rory was very good at tracking dates and schedules, especially other people's.

"Long story." Tina squeezed past Rory and grabbed a drink from the mini-fridge. "What brings you here? Did you come for the booty call?"

Rory gave her a dirty look. "No." Rory didn't run away screaming. Booty call could be a no-no word, but it was also on the sometimes-okay list. She swiveled to face the monitor, clicked the mouse a few times, then swiveled around again. "Everything is booked and confirmed," she said. "It's so much easier to use the dropdown menus on your big computer. The resort's website is buggy as H-E-C-K." Rory could say the word *heck*, but she preferred spelling it out for dramatic emphasis.

Rory was talking about the trip she'd been planning for the two of them.

Tina jumped onto the sofa, which also folded out into her bed. She grabbed a throw pillow and got comfortable.

"Rory, don't take this the wrong way, but wouldn't you rather take a boy with you?"

"Boys are yucky," she said, sounding like she was ten, and not twenty-nine like Tina.

They'd been through Rory's issues a thousand times. She wasn't into girls, and she did like the idea of dating a guy eventually, but not yet. She couldn't even watch R-rated movies. It was a quirk that Tina tried to accept.

"Speaking of boys, I met one today," Tina said. "Not a boy, actually, but a man. He had the biggest hands."

Rory scowled.

Tina continued, "His name is Luca Lowell. He's the guy who bought Ralph's Garage. He's turning it into a bike repair shop."

"You mean for bicycles?"

"No. Bikes." Tina made vroom-vroom gestures with both hands. "Like Harleys and stuff."

"That does sound like something a man would do. Are you interested in going out with him?"

"Not likely. I'm only mentioning it to you because it was the only thing interesting that happened today."

Rory was tapping away on the keyboard. "Luca Lowell. Found him."

Tina sat up straight in alarm, causing the springs in the sofa to protest. "Rory! Don't you dare stalk him. Not on my computer."

"He won't know, as long as we don't click on anything." She started clicking.

"Stop it! Stop clicking!"

She went back to typing. "His photos must be set as private. There. I requested access."

"As me?"

"Of course not. I'm logged in under my secret account that I use for stalking." She paused, staring at the screen. Her posture slumped. "Oops. Don't kill me, but I think this is your profile."

"Undo!" Tina yelled from the couch. "Undo! Undo! Command Z!"

The computer made a sound. Rory clicked a notification icon. "Too late. He already accepted."

Tina muttered to herself, "I need to hide my spare key somewhere better than inside a plastic rock."

"Don't freak out," Rory said, which was ironic as H-E-C-K, coming from the Queen of Freaking Out herself. "Here's the good news. You two have a dozen friends in common already, mostly people from the businesses on Baker Street."

"That's bad news, Rory. That means it's him for sure, and not some other Luca Lowell."

"If he asks, you can tell him it's for business networking."

Tina glared at her best friend, who was moving down the most-loved list to a spot below her sister.

"This isn't fair at all," Tina said. "You freak out if I make one little suggestion about your love life, but it's fair game for you to go chasing after boys with my account? And not just boys, but actual grown men who run businesses and probably have a savings account?"

"It was an accident," she said. "Besides, what's wrong with having a few more friends?"

Tina narrowed her eyes at Rory, as if to say, *I will burn you to the ground.*

Rory widened her eyes, as if to say, *Bring it. I've got the firehose.*

Oh, but Tina could bring it. She could have Rory beat with just one word. Not *booty*. Not even the words for private parts. No. This was war.

Tina warmed up her mouth then said, "Panties."

Rory's face went pale. She froze then awkwardly jumped up from the swivel chair.

"You didn't," she said. "You. Did. Not."

Yes. She. Had.

And there was more. Tina pulled together more of Rory's no-no words and strung them together like artillery fire. "Rory, don't get your panties in a bunch. Let's Netflix and chill. I've got a craving for some *moist* chocolate cake. Would you like to go out for some *moist* chocolate cake?"

Rory grabbed her coat and purse. "Whatever. I need to get packed for our trip, anyway. Don't get mad at me. You shouldn't leave your account logged in by default. It's bad computer security."

"You'd better get out of here before I drop the nuclear bomb."

Rory's eyes widened as she backed up toward the door. "You wouldn't."

"You shouldn't have sent that request to Luca."

She stared back at me. "If you say that word, Tina Gardenia, you'll need to make yourself a new best friend, and it's not going to be easy to replace me."

Tina pursed her lips, raised her eyebrows, then said the word. *That* word. The one that was a euphemism for a body part. Not the British one. Too far! It was the one that meant cat, but not the word cat.

Rory covered her ears with both hands and ran out of the tiny house, howling.

Chapter 4

After stewing about it all night, Tina called Rory on Thursday morning before work.

"I'm sorry I overreacted," Tina said. "I don't know what got into me yesterday, but I'm not mad at you. Please don't be mad at me forever. I'll have to send you flowers at work, and I know you hate that."

"I'm not mad," Rory said. "I would have canceled our trip if I was mad."

"You're not mad?"

"Of course not. I was the one who was meddling. I should have been more careful on your computer."

"I accept your apology, and I'm sorry for saying the p-word."

There was a pause, then Rory asked, "Did you get any messages from your new friend?"

"No. Nothing. And Luca's profile is weirdly bare. It looks like he only uses the account for business. He's been posting a bit about preparing for the garage's grand re-opening, but not much else."

"How did you say you met him?"

"He was in the shop, buying flowers for someone. I assume it was for his girlfriend. He said it was for a woman, and she was mad at him because he did some sort of thing he always does."

There was a pause. She was still there, but not talking.

"I wonder what he did," Tina said, talking to herself as much as to Rory. "He told me he was going to keep doing it, whatever it was."

On the other end of the call, Rory made a strangled sound then said, "I don't know if I can talk about this."

"Why? Do you think it was a sex thing? Like he was in bed with her, and he did some sort of thing that offended her? I can't even imagine. Actually, I can imagine. I'm imagining all sorts of things."

There was silence on the other end of the line.

She held the phone away from her ear. The call had ended. Rory had probably hung up as soon as she'd said the word sex.

Tina sent her a text message apologizing for crossing Rory's boundaries less than thirty seconds after being forgiven, and then headed off to work.

Thursday went by like a typical Thursday. Tina got a postcard from an old high school friend, saying that the honeymoon was great. The friend was one of several that had gotten hitched that year already, and there were more Save-the-Dates coming up.

On Friday, another friend dropped into the flower shop to show off her new baby. He was twelve pounds of adorable.

Even while the girls chatted, Tina kept watching the door, hoping Luca would stop in.

When she was alone, Tina used the office computer to check Luca's social media profile for updates. Nothing happened all day. As for his relationship status, that part of his profile was empty, so there were no clues to be found in the present, or, scrolling deep into his photo history, in his past. There were lots of pictures of bikes, but not much else.

What kind of a woman would Luca Lowell date? Probably a hot blonde. With curves in all the right places. All Tina needed was a wig and some padding. And that scooter she'd been meaning to buy.

Tina helped several teens with their prom flower orders, on both Thursday and Friday, and she didn't break down in tears either of those days. She also didn't notice. It was hard for a person to notice the absence of something, even if that something was a bottomless pit of sorrow.

On Saturday morning, Tina's alarm clock went off early. She didn't have to work at the flower shop that day, but she did have to hit the road. It was the beginning of her weekend getaway at a hot springs resort with her best friend.

Rory had won the getaway package—not cheap!—through a local radio contest. The girls had talked about Rory selling it for cash, but Rory wanted to go and see how the rich and fabulous spent their time.

Tina drove, picking Rory up in her car, and then Tina insisted on paying for all the gas plus the snacks they'd eat on the road.

They were both excited about the getaway. It was such an adult thing to do, going somewhere and paying for a place to sleep when you already had a perfectly good bed at home.

Tina only thought about Luca Lowell about a hundred times on the drive.

They checked in at the resort before noon.

The place was called Dragonfly Resort, and it was owned by the famous action movie star, Jocko Ranger. The handsome, dark-haired actor had filmed a movie there seventeen years earlier. The official story was that Jocko had loved the place so much that he bought it from the owners, who were wanting to retire, as an investment.

The *unofficial* story, according to the gossipy woman at the check-in counter, was that Jocko had thrown some very wild parties toward the end of production. The ensuing damage had been so extensive that he'd been advised by his lawyers to purchase the place mainly to keep from being sued.

Then, since the place was already damaged, Jocko had used it as his personal party spot for the next year, hosting parties for anyone and everyone famous in the surrounding area. Jade, the famous pop singer, was there frequently during that era, among others. Lana Langtree, the internationally renowned country music legend, had even showed up. There had been a spectacular fight between Lana and Jade, who was the country singer's daughter-in-law.

After a year of nonstop parties, Jocko lost interest and moved on to something new. He footed the bill for an extensive renovation, took on a business partner to run the place as an actual business, and now Dragonfly Resort was a popular and busy wellness spa.

Tina and Rory thanked the checkout clerk for the colorful backstory, and went straight for lunch.

Rory said she'd go with Tina into the hot springs after they ate, but that she wouldn't use the spa treatments that had come with the package.

Rory wasn't just squeamish about people talking about bodily functions or sex. Another issue was she couldn't stand people touching her. Rory had to cut her own hair, and she always took a Valium before dentist appointments, if she went at all.

Since Rory wouldn't partake in the treatments, that meant double the massages and pedicures for Tina, which she didn't mind.

For Tina, the rest of Saturday passed in a fog of well-oiled bliss. Those spa people worked her over like taffy on a hot day, and she loved it.

That night, on her rented bed, she slept like a log —a log who dreamed about a certain wavy-haired bike garage owner. She dreamed about all the things he might have done to annoy another woman, but that she wouldn't mind at all.

At brunch on Sunday, Tina had no choice but to keep her vivid dreams to herself. If Rory knew even half of what she'd been thinking about, Rory would have imploded.

After brunch, the girls returned to the double room, and Tina got ready for her daily massage treatment—she could get used to this!—while Rory got ready for the steam room. Rory was actually opening up a little. She was willing to be in a swimsuit, near other women in their swimsuits.

Tina told Rory, "I'm so proud of you. And that swimsuit is cute."

"Don't you dare take a picture," Rory said.

"I wasn't going to." That wasn't true. She'd been planning to. "I'm not even touching my phone." A likely story.

Rory checked out the view of her back in the room's full-length mirror. "I hope the steam room is as relaxing as people say it is. You were making weird noises in your sleep, and you woke me up."

"Sorry," Tina said.

"What were you dreaming about?"

"Waffles," Tina lied.

They went off to their separate treatments.

When Tina got to the treatment room, she was greeted by a perky young woman whose name she immediately forgot. Tina was given her choice of massage therapists.

"Denise is off today so you can't have her," said the perky young woman. "That's who you had yesterday. Denise is just terrific! I love her! Don't you love her? Of course you do! So, for today, I can get you in with almost anyone, since it's pretty quiet this afternoon." She looked over the screen of a tablet. "What sort of energy would you like to be around?"

Slightly less perky than you, Tina thought. And then, perhaps because she was still thinking about the previous night's dreams, she made a joke, saying, "I'll take the one with the biggest hands."

Perky Spa Chick tapped at her tablet. "Terrific! He will be with you in a moment."

"He will be?" Emphasis on the word *he*. All her massages and treatments up until that point had been given by females.

Perky Spa Chick said, "Please make yourself comfortable on the table. Relax." Then she gave Tina a funny little smile, as though Perky Spa Chick knew what Tina had been thinking about and dreaming about. It hadn't been waffles.

Tina waited, alone and nearly naked on a treatment table. She did anything *but* relax. Her brain badgered her with worries, and she began berating herself. *Tina, now you've done it! Perky Spa Chick thinks you want a happy ending. Why'd you have to ask for someone with big hands? Aren't the dreams enough for you? What if the spa puts you on some sort of registered pervert list?*

She watched the treatment room door with dread while coming up with excuses to get out of there. She could tell them her stomach was upset from eating bad fish last night. But then the rumor about food poisoning might get back to the kitchen, who'd report that they didn't serve any fish last night, let alone to Tina. Then Perky Spa Chick would know Tina was both a pervert and a compulsive liar.

So she stayed, waiting on the table. Still nearly naked.

Tina began to get curious about this massage therapist with big hands. What would that even feel like? The guys she'd dated usually had hands not much bigger than hers. She was tall, at five foot nine, and her boyfriends had never been particularly tall. Half of them had been shorter than her.

There were sounds on the other side of the treatment room door.

Tina imagined a mystery guy getting ready, washing his big hands and complaining to his coworkers about having to give *yet another happy ending* to a horny spa guest. "These rich old ladies think everyone is on the menu," he'd say, rolling his eyes at his coworker and part-time lover, Perky Spa Chick.

The door to the treatment room squeaked open, and someone slipped in quietly. Tina heard very soft footsteps. Was the massage therapist wearing slippers, or was the issue that she couldn't hear anything over the pounding of her pulse in her ears? She lifted her head to take a peek.

It was a *he*, all right. Big hands and all. The man looked like an Olympic skier from Norway. His square jaw and blue eyes reminded her of Luca.

She put her face down into the table's padded supports and tried to calmly breathe her way out of a heart attack. Could people have heart attacks at twenty-nine? She'd hate to make the news for something like that.

Tina, you're going to survive this, she told herself. *Now, I know you've had some weird ideas on your brain, but I have a simple request. Whatever happens next, please promise you will not moan. This man is a professional, and he's going to give you a professional massage. Keep your mouth shut and keep your happy sounds to yourself. Do you hear me, Tina's body? No wiggling around under his touch.*

The Norwegian Olympian said, "My name is Daniel, by the way. The ladies call me Big Danny the Manny, or just Big Danny."

"I'll bet they do." Tina kept her face down, her eyes safely on the tiled floor beneath them.

Big Danny the Manny asked, "Are you enjoying your stay?"

"Yes," she squeaked out. "Very much. I'm here with my girlfriend."

He chuckled. "Girlfriend, hmm?" He sounded very interested. That gave her an idea.

She pulled her face up from the pads and turned to face Daniel. "Yes, my *girlfriend*," she said, with a heavy emphasis on the word *girlfriend*. "Her name is Rory, and she's very jealous. She doesn't like that I've been getting so many massages from other girls. That's the only reason I requested a guy today."

"Oh." He sounded crestfallen. "I was told you asked for me by name. I thought you heard about me by reputation. I thought you wanted Big Danny the Manny."

"Uh, no. Uh, what reputation?"

"You'll see." He gathered up some bottles of oil and set them on a rolling tray next to the massage table. "Head down and relax."

She tried. Her head wouldn't even go down, let alone relax. She stared at him, wide eyed, as he rubbed the oil on his hands.

"You can tell your *girlfriend* all about your special relaxation time with Big Danny," he said, with a heavy emphasis on the word *girlfriend*. Did he say it that way to let her know he thought she was fibbing? And what did he mean by *special relaxation time*? And why *did* the ladies call him Big Danny the Manny?

She finally returned her face to the oval-shaped hole in the padding and tried to relax. *Tina, do not sigh, and do not think about Luca Lowell. When Big*

Danny touches you, do not imagine those are Luca's paint-speckled hands on your lower back.

Big Danny got to work, explaining each part of the massage as he went.

"You have some areas of tension," he said.

"Oh?" Her voice sounded awkward, with her cheeks squeezed by the pads.

"You're going to put me through my paces. Hang on, you're going for a ride."

Hang on? Hang on to what? What ride?

Something whirred, and the table lowered, moving a foot closer to the ground.

"Much better," he said. "Now I can really get in there."

She could only see the floor, but she scrunched her eyes shut anyway. What was happening? There was no way Big Danny had been through formal training as a massage therapist. She'd been to a few RMTs. None of them said things like *get in there,* or *hang on,* or *you're going for a ride.*

"You're so tense," he murmured.

His hands were on her shoulders. She understood what he meant. Her shoulders did carry a lot of tension. And yet, by some miracle, the muscles began to ease under his skilled pressure. She felt some of the stress she perpetually carried falling away. That was a change.

"Feel free to vocalize," he said.

"Hmm?"

"You can vocalize if you'd like," he said. "Some women find it helps them relax."

"Very good work," she said quickly, thinking he was asking for compliments. "Yes. Thank you. I am enjoying this massage exactly how it's going, thank you."

"That's not what I meant, but you're welcome." Big Danny chuckled and kept working.

His fingers worked the muscles between her shoulders. Just when the pressure started to become too much, and she feared she might be bruising like a ripe peach, he moved down an inch. It got better by the minute. The thing was, the massage she'd gotten from Denise the day before had been perfectly good. Fine. A four-star massage. But Big Danny's hands on her spine were a revelation.

Her whole body felt like it might be glowing.

He moved back up to her shoulders then her upper arms. When his long fingers wrapped around her biceps, his hands felt bigger than ever. She had strong arms from working at the flower shop—there was a surprising amount of heavy lifting—but he made her muscles feel tiny and delicate.

Images of Luca came to mind, then a daydream formed. In the scenario, he was fixing a bike, and there was dark oil on his hands. He looked up when Tina walked in. She wasn't wearing tattered shorts and an enormous sweatshirt. She was dressed in a tight black sweater and sexy black leather pants. She was dressed as the former good girl Sandy at the end of the classic movie musical *Grease*.

Keep in mind this was all happening inside Tina's imagination, where she didn't look at all ridiculous in leather pants.

In the daydream, Luca stood and crossed to the sink to wash his hands. Tina told him not to bother washing up. She couldn't wait to be held by him, and she didn't mind that his hands were dirty.

"Tina, you really know how to fill out those leather pants," he growled.

She said, in classic Sandy-from-Grease style, "Tell me about it, stud."

With his upper lip curling up Travolta style, he grabbed a loose rag and gave his palms a quick wipe as he walked toward her. No. Swaggered. His hands were now magically clean. He reached around and planted both hands on her butt. In her leather pants, her butt looked and felt like a million bucks.

He whispered near her ear, "Your butt feels like a million bucks, Tina Gardenia."

"I know."

And then…

"Are you asleep?" a male voice asked.

Tina's eyes flew open, taking in a limited view of the slate tile floor. She could see Big Danny's feet. He was wearing socks with sandals. She had never, ever, ever been more thrilled to see a pair of socks and sandals. It was, thankfully, a complete and immediate turn-off.

He asked again, "Are you asleep?"

"Not anymore," she said groggily. "Maybe I did drift off."

"You sounded like you were having a good dream. You made some interesting sounds."

She lifted her head up to give him a stern look, taking care not to flash him. "I dreamed I was eating waffles."

"Don't worry," he said, waggling his eyebrows. "I won't tell your girlfriend."

"She was in the dream, too."

Grinning, he walked over to the sink and washed the massage oil off his hands. "Let me know if you need anything else," he said.

She shooed him away with one hand. "You've done more than enough," she said. "Sorry I fell asleep. I guess some people find massages boring."

Big Danny bent over, pulled up the socks he was wearing with his sandals, and then left.

Once he was gone, she sat up and waited for her sinuses to clear. Humans weren't made to lie face-down.

She grabbed her robe and headed to the changing room.

Thanks to Big Danny, she did receive the best massage she'd ever had in her life, but now she was miserable.

She was miserable because, while she earned a reasonable wage at the family flower shop, she couldn't afford the cash to regularly visit the fancy spa for a massage.

As she got dressed, she ran some mental math. Technically, she could afford a session with Big Danny about once a month, if she cut back on shopping.

    * * *

Tina met Rory in the resort's cafe, where Rory was already seated for high tea.

"Your face looks weird." Rory poured her some cinnamon-scented tea.

Tina rubbed her forehead. "These massage-table lines will disappear after I drink some water. I'm probably dehydrated."

"No. I mean you've got a goofy look on your face. It's a look I haven't seen in a long, long time."

Tina used the silver tongs to transfer a tiny cucumber sandwich from the tray to her plate. "Okay," she said, barely paying attention. The food looked good, and she was starving. Tina could have eaten a hundred of the tiny sandwiches. She could have grabbed them by the fistful and stuffed the whole tray's contents into her mouth, Godzilla style. Why were the rooms so big and the food so small? Rich people had different priorities. They liked palatial suites and miniature food.

Rory leaned in and whispered, "Did something happen at your massage?"

"Not exactly, but there was a bit of a surprise. It was a guy this time. Denise is off today."

"A guy?" Rory's eyes widened in terror. "Did he… touch you?"

"Yes, Rory. That's pretty much the definition of a massage. They have to touch you."

"You know what I mean."

"No, he didn't touch my bathing suit area."

Rory made a gagging face, then immediately dropped the subject.

The girls finished their tea, then packed up their suitcases and checked out again.

The weekend had gone by too quickly, they both agreed.

The sun was setting as they started the drive back home.

Tina felt tired but also rejuvenated. Rory's skin looked great from her time in the hot springs and the sauna.

"Thanks for bringing me with you," Tina said once they were on the highway. "I know you could have sold the prize for cash, but I really appreciate you bringing me instead."

Rory was quiet. Tina pulled her eyes off the road to look at her friend.

Rory was crying silently, tears glistening on her cheeks.

Tina's throat tightened. Rory never cried.

"What's wrong?" Tina returned to facing the road, giving her friend some privacy. It was humiliating to be seen crying. Tina knew that from experience.

Rory sniffed. "I didn't win the getaway."

"You what?"

"There was no radio contest," she said.

It sank in for Tina, but not all the way. "What?"

"I bought it myself to cheer you up," Rory said. "Because you always get so sad this time of year."

Tina's eyes burned. Her throat felt tight, and also blocked.

"You didn't have to do that," Tina said softly.

"I know," Rory said. "Don't make fun of me for being a weirdo."

"I'm not."

They drove for a while in silence. The sun was gone. The sky was cool blue, and getting darker.

After a while, Tina said, "Thank you for this weekend, Rory. You know I love you, right?"

Rory sniffed. The crying had stopped, but it hadn't gone far.

"Tina, I feel bad," Rory said. "I think I'm part of the problem. I'm holding you back."

"Don't be silly. What are you talking about? You're holding me back from what?"

"You should have a boyfriend," Rory said. "You're pretty, and smart, and funny. And you don't have some major psychological issue that prevents you from kissing or holding hands. We're almost thirty. Thirty! All our other friends are getting married, having kids. The only reason you're still single is me."

"I wouldn't say that's the *only* reason."

Rory turned and climbed over the seats to get the tissue box from the back window. She returned and blew her nose.

They rolled down the highway in silence. The inside of the car felt cozy compared to the midnight blue around them. Driving was good for talking.

"I need to let you go," Rory said.

Tina laughed nervously. "Rory, are you breaking up with me?"

"We should take some time apart."

"What?" Tina didn't know whether to laugh or cry. She'd been single for a year, and she was still getting dumped? Life wasn't fair.

Rory sniffed again. "Or you could promise me you'll go on some dates," she said. "Maybe once a week. Then I'll know I'm not holding you back."

Tina stared at the dotted yellow line on the highway, thinking over what had been said.

"It's the only way," Rory said.

Tina said nothing.

One of Rory's favorite songs came on the radio.

Tina waited for what she knew would happen next, and it did.

"I love this song," Rory said, turning up the volume.

It was a woman singing a cover of *Fields of Gold*, by Sting. The lyrics were about someone asking to be remembered when they were gone.

The song always reminded Tina of her first love. The boy who gave her blue roses, then died two months after graduation. But that was because every sad song reminded her of him, and some of the happy ones, too.

Whatever was holding her back, she didn't believe it was Rory.

Chapter 5

It was Monday morning, and two weeks had passed since Tina's weekend getaway at the resort with Rory. Two weeks since her massage. She'd been thinking about Big Danny, and his socks and sandals, and his big, magic hands.

Tina was walking down Baker Street on her way to open the flower shop when a sign in a window caught her eye:

Massage Therapist On Duty Monday-Friday

There was a massage therapist working at the local chiropractor's office. But of course there was. There probably always had been, and she hadn't noticed before. That meant she didn't need to drive out to the ritzy hot springs to get a massage.

Tina lingered at the window, trying to get a peek inside. She wondered if the massage therapist was a guy or a girl.

There was a brochure-holder box near the front door, full of brochures and business cards. A bunch of the shops around the area set out material like this, for the people who came by the restaurants in the evening.

Tina was reaching for a card when she heard a deep male voice.

"What on earth are you doing?"

She jerked back her hand guiltily and turned to see Luca Lowell. He was wearing his usual biker boots, jeans, and a plain gray shirt that was straining to contain all of his strength. There was something different about his appearance. Had he gotten more handsome? How was it possible? His hair had grown longer in the last two and a half weeks since they'd met. He was letting more of his waves show, and it suited him. He was also clean-shaven, with kissable smooth cheeks.

One thing hadn't changed. Those bright-blue eyes of his were once again taking Tina's breath away.

If only there had been one thing imperfect about the man, then it might have been easier for her to keep her cool. Why did he have to wear biker boots? Socks with sandals were very comfortable.

Luca tilted his head to one side and narrowed his eyes at the chiropractor's brochure-holder. He asked, "Are you going to tell me what you're doing?"

"I'm not doing anything," she said, defensiveness making her voice rise. "I'm just minding my own business, walking to work."

He straightened his head and gave her a chiding look. "And you don't seem to be in any hurry."

"I'm not in any hurry. Why? Should I be?"

"You've had a customer waiting at your shop for the last ten minutes, waiting for you to open."

She looked down the street at the storefront. Nobody was in front of the flower shop. "That's too bad," she said. "But don't worry. They'll come back."

"They might not," he said, a hint of a grin forming on his lips. "They might take down the five-star review they wrote for your business and put up a bad one."

She finally picked up on what he was getting at. "Was it you?"

"It was me." He pulled his phone from his pocket. "It is now twelve minutes past the opening time posted on your door."

"Those aren't the actual hours," she said. "They're more like guidelines. That's why there's a little star-shaped symbol next to all the times. The hours are flexible."

He gave her a sideways look. "Is that any way to run a business?"

"Sure. It might not be the perfect way to run a business, but it's *a* way."

"You're good with words," he said. "I bet you play a mean game of Scrabble."

"I can hold my own."

He tilted his head again, and the brown waves of his hair caught the light perfectly. "Are we going to stand in front of the chiropractor's office all day, or are you going to sell me some of your pretty flowers?"

She plucked a card for massages from the display then started walking. "Right this way, sir. Mr. Customer, sir."

He walked beside her to the end of the block. They waited without talking for the light to change before crossing the street. It was a gorgeous day. The morning sun hit the planes of Luca's face, turning it into a masterpiece to match his hair. He was what Tina and Megan's mother would call a Golden Boy. When Tina was growing up, she thought her mother said that to compare people to golden retrievers, but, as of that morning, she understood it. When the sunshine hit him, Luca was radiant. He was a Golden Boy.

As they crossed the street, he asked, "What have you been up to, Flower Shop Girl?"

"You don't remember my name."

"Sure I do. I just didn't want to wear it out too soon." He paused. "Tina."

A shiver went down her spine.

He pointed to the card in her hands. "Are you in the market for a massage?"

"That depends. Are you offering?"

"Er." He loosely smacked one big hand against his cheek. "C'mon, Luca," he told himself. "That's what you get for asking stupid questions."

"It wasn't that stupid," she said.

He smiled.

They reached the door to the flower shop. She pulled out her keys and, by some miracle, managed to get the door open without dropping them.

Luca followed her into the cool interior.

"Chilly," he said. "Brr."

She laughed.

"What?" He gave her a puzzled look. "Is the heater broken?"

"It's just funny to hear a big, tough guy like you say the word *chilly*, and then *brr*."

"Big, tough guys have feelings, too," he said. "Big, tough guys can get chilly."

They walked past the ferns, which had been pushed back to widen the aisle since Luca's last visit, but still tickled Tina's bare arms. She was wearing a flower-print sundress and gladiator-style sandals. It was a major upgrade from the grubby duds she'd been wearing the first time they'd met.

Luca said, "I'll have to watch what I say around you. I'll stick to big-tough-guy words, like *bullets*, and *barbed wire*, and *battleships*."

She flicked on the lights and pivoted to face him.

"Bullets, barbed wire, and battleships? You could put those three things together and make a great tattoo."

He raised his eyebrows and nodded. "That's a good idea, but I don't believe in tattoos."

"What are you talking about?" She reached out and squeezed his forearm, which she could have sworn had tattoos, but didn't. "How can a guy like you not believe in tattoos?"

He looked down at her hand on his arm.

"That's funny," she said. "I could have sworn you had tattoos."

His eyes flicked up from her hand to her face. "I've got nothing against other people's choices, but I prefer my skin exactly how it is," he said evenly.

She gave his forearm a light squeeze before pulling her hand away.

"You do have nice skin," she said. "I guess some people don't need anything else. Some people are already perfect, exactly how they are."

He walked over to the sliding doors that ran across the walk-in cooler. "I'm not perfect," he said, his back to her. "Far from it. Which is why I'm here today. I need more of those apology flowers."

"Already? It's only been a couple weeks since your last one."

"Different woman."

She swallowed hard. The only thing worse than learning Luca had a girlfriend was learning that he had two.

She pulled down some vases from the upper shelves behind the counter and set them out. Then she grabbed some of the freshest-looking blossoms from the last auction and started trying color combinations.

Luca watched quietly, not offering more information.

"You're a busy guy, dating two women at once," she said.

"You think I'm dating two women? Is that what you wanted to know about when you followed me on social media?"

So he *had* logged in, and he *had* noticed. Tina had been hoping he'd been too busy with his renovation to take much notice.

"My friend Rory did that," she said, as casually as she could manage. "She was messing around on my computer. It was an accident. She was going to unfollow you right away, but that's so rude."

"Is it? I don't really do social media or any of that kid stuff."

"Good. Then you didn't see my profile, with all my embarrassing photos."

"I wouldn't say that." He paused, savoring the moment. "I was expecting more pictures of your bouquets, but all you post are pictures of a cat."

"That's not just any cat. That's Muffins. He's a great cat. Possibly the *best* cat."

"What's Muffins like?"

"For one thing, he does *not* like taking a bath. He does love tuna. His favorite activities are sleeping in sunbeams and hiding twist-ties in people's shoes."

Luca leaned over to take a close look at the peach-colored roses between them. "To answer your earlier implication, no. I would never date two women at once. Even just dating one takes up so much time." He pointed to the cobalt-blue vase. "This one will do."

Tina grabbed a knife and whittled away at a green insert so it would fit in the vase. What had he meant about one woman taking up so much time? She didn't like Luca saying things like that. She wanted to live in a world where guys like Luca were committed and loving, even if it wasn't with her. She had to say something.

"Luca, the thing is…" She changed her mind and trailed off. What was the point?

"The thing is what? Dating advice?" He stretched out his arms. "Hit me. I'm genuinely interested. You do a great job running a business, showing up at whatever-o'clock. I can't wait to hear more of your wisdom."

She worried she'd offended him, but then she saw the twinkle in his eyes. He was giving her a hard time. Which was great. She'd rather get a hard time from Luca Lowell than any other sort of a time from anyone else.

"Don't hold back now," he said. "I won't tell anyone in the neighborhood that you're giving counseling over here without a license. You and I have florist-client confidentiality."

"Counseling is more my sister's thing." She nodded at the office door. Again, it would have made more sense if Meenie had actually been there.

She stabbed the green insert a few more times then dropped it in the vase.

"Spit it out," he said.

"Well... if you really care about someone, they're not *taking up* your time. Sitting in traffic takes up your time. Waiting in line at the bank to get change takes up your time. But being around someone you care about is a gift. If there's ever a time they're not around anymore, you'll wish you'd had more time to give them."

His eyebrows bunched together. He stared steadily into her with those sky-blue eyes.

"Or something like that," she said with a throw-away shrug.

"How did you get to be so wise, Flower Shop Girl?"

"I don't know."

"I think you do."

"Okay." She felt the cold-fingered touch of the sorrow inside her that never went away. If he had to know, she'd tell him. "There was a time I knew someone who didn't have much time, and he chose to spend all of it with the people he loved."

Luca took a step back, pushed his hands into his jean pockets, and looked down at his boots. "All right, then," he said. "I have been told."

"I didn't mean to make you feel bad," she said. "I'm the worst. You came here for flowers, and I kept you waiting, then I gave you a lecture. I truly am the worst business person on the whole street. You should probably keep your distance from me before everyone else finds out about us."

He squinted. "Finds out about us?"

"Being friends," she said. "Online."

"Online," he said, nodding. "Friends."

The door chimed, and one of Gardenia Flowers' regular customers came in.

Now that they had an audience, Tina put on her professional florist face. "When do you need the arrangement ready by, Mr. Lowell?"

Luca glanced over his shoulder then back at her, grinning. "Mr. Lowell? For a minute, I thought my dad had just walked in."

"Just trying to salvage what's left of our florist-client relationship," she said. "When do you need the flowers?"

"How about closing time again? You're here until six?"

She wouldn't be there, but forgot to say so in the moment. "I'll have your order ready before then, Mr. Lowell. Would you like anything written on a card?"

He tossed his chin upward defiantly. "I would like... *the usual*."

He turned and walked out.

The other customer was still looking around, so Tina pulled out a note card and wrote the usual: SORRY I'M A JERK. - LUCA

She creased the card and tucked it into an envelope.

She wondered what he'd done this time.

Chapter 6

Wednesday morning, Tina Gardenia hustled to get all the flower orders done quickly so she could take her break.

On her way in that morning, she'd bought a bag of chewy candies and two trashy gossip magazines that she intended to read from cover to cover. It was what passed for excitement in Tina's life.

Once her customers were all taken care of, she let out a sigh of satisfaction and pulled the stool up to the counter.

She settled in and flipped open the magazine cover.

She hadn't started reading yet when the front door chimed.

Luca Lowell came in, looking unhappy. Handsome, as always, but unhappy. The Golden Boy was the Cloudy Boy, or the Cloudy Man.

"I have a complaint to lodge," he said.

"Oh? Your lady friend didn't like the arrangement I made you on Monday?"

"She loved it." He kept frowning. This was a new side of him, and she didn't like it. She felt guilty. Had she messed up the bouquet? It had been even more spectacular than the first one. Way over budget, and she had barely charged him anything. The flower shop was going to lose money that month if she kept trying so hard to impress Luca's girlfriends, but she couldn't help herself.

"And?" Tina waved to the magazine that lay on the counter between them. "As you can see, this article about trouble with the Royal Family isn't going to read itself." She leaned forward and whispered, "The Royals are just like regular folks. They do not get along, and the younger ones have all sorts of ideas about how things should be done differently. They're always trying to change things that have been perfectly good for generations."

Luca blinked at her and ignored everything about the Royal family. "My complaint is that my preferred florist wasn't here on Monday at closing."

"That's normal. My sister and I share all the shifts here. She took over after lunch that day. Did she do something wrong? Say something awful? She was probably just making a joke. Some people don't get her humor." Tina winced. "Not some people, but most people. Her sense of humor can be hard to receive. Her name is Megan, but everyone calls her Meenie for a reason."

"Your sister was perfectly nice, and professional."

"Really? Are you sure you were here, and not some other flower shop?"

"She wasn't perfect, but she wasn't too bad," he said. "But my complaint is that she's not you."

"We do share a lot of genetic material. We are sisters. Therefore, she's far more like me than any of the other people on this planet. Compared to those other people, she's practically the same as me. So, what's your complaint?"

"You heard me."

"I don't have a time machine," she said. "And I'm not going to start working eighty hours a week just so I can be here at all times."

He stared at her steadily. "If she's such a good substitution for you, then I should ask your sister to go out on a date."

Tina looked down and pretended to read the article about trouble at Buckingham Palace.

"Sure," she said. "Ask away. I don't think she's seeing anyone right now. Not since the last one ran for the hills, changed his name, and then faked his own death."

"Your sister doesn't sound like such a catch."

"That's why I'm always trying to throw her in as a bonus bride."

"Why all the talk about weddings? Are you getting married soon, Flower Shop Girl?"

"Not that I know of. I have been getting a lot of save-the-date invites lately, though. I suppose I should check for my name."

He stared at her steadily. "You've already got your bridal flowers planned out, haven't you?"

"No," she said, which wasn't entirely true. "The only thing I have planned out is a bunch of future dental work, from eating all this junk." Tina picked up her bag of chewy candies and offered him a piece.

"Oh," he said. "Do you have a dentist appointment on Friday?"

"Not that I know of."

"Then you're free," he said. "Come out with me for drinks."

"What kind of drinks?" She kept her gaze down on her magazine. If she looked into Luca's striking blue eyes, she'd get lost.

"Networking drinks," he said. "Two local business owners getting together to swap tips. You were right about the folks around here hating me. They're all irate about losing their service garage."

"Told you so."

"I've been thinking, since you have the remarkable ability to spot all my many shortcomings a mile away, we can get some drinks, and you can tell me everything I'm doing wrong."

"Sure. You don't even need to ply me with liquor to get my tips. For one thing, don't change the name of the shop."

"I don't understand."

"It's called Ralph's Garage. And your new business is a garage, right?"

"Yes."

"My advice is that you keep calling the place Ralph's Garage. Add on a smaller sign saying you specialize in bikes. You can keep doing some oil changes and light maintenance on cars for a few years, until people get used to you. It's not going to happen overnight. Folks around here don't jump on every trend that comes and goes. That's why the cupcake shops and the churro hut are gone. You'll probably do just fine, but even a well-run business that opens on time takes some time to get established."

"You've given this a lot of thought."

"This neighborhood is my whole life."

"Should I change my name to Ralph, just so I don't alarm any of the folks who don't appreciate new ideas?"

"It wouldn't hurt."

"I'm not changing my name to Ralph. And I'm opening a garage for bikes, not cars."

"Eventually you'll just do bikes. Like I said, it's not going to happen overnight. When you do get too busy for cars, find some other places to refer the business to. Don't just tell folks to look in the phone book or research a place online. They hate that. Get out and try some other garages yourself, until you find one you like, and then refer people to a place or two that you personally vouch for. Like Ralph's, but a slightly longer drive across town. If you ease people in, they'll appreciate it."

He was quiet for a moment then said, "You're a savvy business person, even if your posted hours are unreliable."

She glanced up at his gorgeous face. The combination of his good looks and his compliments about her business school made her head go blank. What had they been talking about?

"Forget about networking drinks," he said gruffly. "You've already given me my money's worth. I'll have to buy you dinner. Anything you want. Dinner on Friday?"

"Friday's no good. I'm always busy on Fridays." That was as big a lie as any Tina Gardenia had ever uttered inside the flower shop. Even bigger than telling a customer she *liked* daffodils. Horrible flowers.

"Busy," he mused. "Your sister said you'd be free, but she must have forgotten to check your social media. I've been checking, and I've noticed that Friday night is when you put bow-ties on that kooky cat of yours and take photos of him looking disgruntled."

"That's how he always looks."

"Muffins can take a night off," he said. "I'm flexible. We could get an early dinner, or a late one. I'll work around your busy schedule."

"Maybe some other time."

"Today's Wednesday," he said. "You have two days to think it over. I know I'll be thinking about it. Dinner on Friday."

She chewed her lower lip. Why wasn't she saying yes? Was it because the Luca in her imagination was so much easier to handle than Luca in real life? The one in her daydreams didn't lodge complaints about her not being there, or question her truthfulness about Friday night plans. And how did Luca know she'd picked up a new bow-tie for Muffins?

Luca took the bag of candies from her hand then plucked out a half dozen of the fuzzy peaches. That was all of the fuzzy peaches that came in one bag.

"Hey! Those are the best ones," she said. "All you're leaving me with are blue sharks and whatever those other things are. Mushrooms?"

He put three fuzzy peaches in his mouth, then another three. "Mmm."

"Real mature."

He gave her a wide grin. His teeth were covered in peach-colored candies. Then he turned and walked out, boots thudding on the floor.

She stared after him helplessly. His butt looked so good in his jeans that she wished he'd walk slower. If only she hadn't pushed back the fern jungle and made the aisle so wide.

The door closed behind him.

Tina stuffed some blue sharks in her mouth.

What just happened?

First of all, she had been robbed of her fuzzy peaches.

Second, Luca Lowell had asked her out on a date. He'd made it sound like it would be about business, but then like it wasn't.

She smacked her hands to her face. She hadn't exactly said yes to him.

What was wrong with her? Besides everything.

The door chimed, and Tina's sister walked in. Megan didn't even say hello before diving for the bag of candy. "You ate all the peaches," she said.

"Luca Lowell ate them."

"Who?"

"A customer. The guy who took over Ralph's Garage. He came in today, and he didn't even buy flowers. He asked me out for drinks. No. He upgraded it to dinner because I gave him some business advice."

"You? Giving advice?" Megan snorted. "Poor guy."

"You're a monster."

"I know." Megan gave her sister side-eye. "He was asking me about you when he picked up his flowers Monday. We are talking about the super-hot guy with the motorcycle boots?"

"That's the one."

"He's really big," Megan said, stuffing more candies in her mouth. "He's too big for one girl. You should share him with me."

"Ew. Why do you have to be like that?" Tina pulled away the candy bag before her sister ate them all.

"I'm just kidding. Take a joke, Teenie! He's all yours." Megan wrinkled her nose. "He's not really my type." She stole the candies back. "When are you going on this date? I told him you're free anytime, if he can drag you away from Rory. Don't worry. I didn't tell him about how weird you two are together. I didn't want to scare him off."

"Thanks. I think we're going out Friday, but I'm not sure I said yes."

Megan looked thoughtful for a minute. "Okay. Yup. That makes sense. Of course you didn't say yes. You don't know what's good for you." She yawned and started looking over the new floral display by the counter. She pointed to the fresh-cut parrot tulips on display and changed the topic. "Those are gorgeous, but you can't put yellow and red together."

"Of course you can."

"No, you can't. It makes people think of ketchup and mustard. Like on hot dogs."

"Maybe yellow and red do that for you, but you don't speak for all customers."

Megan gave her sister a *duh* look. "Uh, I think I know what people like, Teenie. I've only been in this business for, like, ever."

"Fine." Tina started separating the yellow and red tulips. The yellow ones had red bases. The flowers did go well together. Megan was just crazy and stubborn about, well, lots of things.

Megan slurped noisily on the candies. Tina's sister was a loud eater. She was loud in a lot of ways.

After a moment, Tina asked, "What do you mean I don't know what's good for me? Ever since you got into self-help, you think you're the expert on everyone else. You're always acting like there's something wrong with me."

Megan picked up the magazine and leafed through it. "There's nothing wrong with you that can't be fixed. I'm actually glad you're cautious. We don't know anything about this Luca guy. He could be a serial killer."

"Serial killer? I don't think so. He's probably just a garden-variety jerk."

Megan looked up from the magazine, her eyes crinkling at the edges with her smile. "At least he buys flowers. That's always a good sign. There are far worse guys out there than the ones who buy flowers."

"Except he's been buying apology flowers for a woman who was mad at him about something." Tina coughed and corrected herself, finger in the air. "Technically, two different women."

The crinkle left Megan's eyes. "Ouch."

"Exactly."

Tina started gathering her purse and things so she could go home to Muffins. Luca was wrong about one thing. She didn't spend Friday nights dressing up her cat and taking his photo. That was something she could do any night of the week.

Megan flipped through the magazine. "Oh, Meghan Markle. You're a disgrace to the Megan brand. What have you done now? Tsk, tsk."

"Do you think Luca's out of my league?" Tina asked. "Do you think I could actually date him? Assuming that whatever he did to have to buy those flowers for other women wasn't too bad, and that he's not seeing them anymore."

"Luca Lowell? He's not in your league, Teenie. He's not in anyone's league. He's in his *own* league."

That wasn't the answer Tina was hoping for. Her insides twisted up. Inside Tina's brain, the well-worn neurological pathway for yelling at her sister lit up with green lights at every intersection.

"Meenie! Why'd you have to open your big mouth and talk him into asking me out if you don't think I even have a chance?"

"Me? I didn't do anything. He was the one asking all the questions."

"That's not how it sounded when he told me about it. It sounded like you were playing matchmaker."

Megan pointed at her sister. "This is called transference. You're upset about something else, and you're taking it out on me, the innocent bystander."

Tina told her sister where to take all her therapy talk, then Tina started walking out. Storming out. In a huff.

Megan reached out with her wrestler speed and grabbed Tina's arm to stop her, mid-huff. "Tina," she said, using her sister's real name to show she wasn't messing around, for a change. "All I meant by saying he's in his own league is that he's not your *usual* type. He doesn't look like he collects trading cards and superhero figurines. He might not even live with his mother."

Tina shook her arm away from her sister's grasp. "Whatever. I heard what you said, loud and clear." She resumed storming out of the shop in a huff. There were some casualties in the fern jungle, with a few dropped fronds.

Megan called after Tina, but only half-heartedly, and with a mouth full of Tina's candies.

Chapter 7

Thursday morning, Tina Gardenia was shocked when she opened the flower shop and found it looking very different from how she'd left it the previous afternoon.

Her first thought was that they'd been robbed. What else could explain it? The cooler shelves had been stripped bare of flowers. The fern jungle was a desert wasteland. Only a few potted plants remained. What kind of a thief stole flowers?

She ran to check the cash register. It wasn't exactly full of money, but that was normal for the morning. The float was still there.

The slot where the sisters kept receipts was stuffed full of paper—all receipts dated from the previous afternoon. There were multiple transactions, so it hadn't been a bulk order from another shop.

Had Wednesday been some holiday or annual event she'd forgotten about? She checked the calendar. No holiday. Just a regular Wednesday.

Had they run an advertisement or done one of those group coupon deals? She hated those coupon deals. They were supposed to be good for businesses, but what good was losing money on every order? She pulled out her phone and called her sister.

"What?" Megan sounded sleepy.

"What happened here yesterday? I thought we'd been robbed."

Megan snickered.

"Meenie, if the store was getting slammed, why didn't you call me to come in and help? I would have come in, you dummy. You sold everything in here, all by yourself?"

"What can I say? I'm a spectacular salesperson."

"Yeah, right. Was it a last-minute big event? No. It couldn't have been that, because then you wouldn't have all these little receipts."

Megan snorted with laughter. "You don't know, do you?"

Tina yelled into the phone, "MEENIE!"

Megan yelled back, "TEENIE."

"You're not going to tell me, are you?"

"I'm going back to sleep. Have a nice day!"

Tina put her phone away and pulled out the box of phone numbers for suppliers. She had to get more flowers in, before their regular delivery from the auction.

The door chimed, and in walked Luca Lowell. Unlike the last visit, he wasn't cranky or frowning. With a big grin on his face, he was the walking embodiment of Mr. Sunshine.

"You're welcome," he said.

She waved at the empty shelves. "You did this? You stole all my flowers? I should have known."

"Nobody stole anything."

He leaned on the counter casually. He hadn't shaved in a few days, and there was reddish-brown hair dotting his square jaw. His wavy brown hair curled around his ears. There was something about his scruffiness that made her want to touch him, even more than when he was clean-shaven.

"Put that away," he said, pointing to the supplier cards in her hands. "Your sister already super-sized the new order that's coming in Friday morning. She's a funny one, your sister."

"Megan?" Tina snorted. "Yeah, she's really funny."

"She told me your nicknames are Teenie and Meenie. That's cute, and I'm not a man who uses the word *cute* lightly."

"Sounds like you and Megan are best friends now. What exactly happened here yesterday afternoon?"

He scratched his scruffy chin, acting comfortable and casual around her. Tina, however, was standing tall and rigid, with her arms crossed sternly. She realized this and tried to look a little less defensive and angry. She uncrossed her arms then recrossed them behind her back.

Luca took in a deep breath and explained, "All my guys have been working hard to get the renovations at the garage done. Their wives and girlfriends haven't been too happy. Yesterday, I told them they could knock off early. But only if they walked across the street to the best-run flower shop in town and picked up something to bring home."

"This was you? I mean, your construction guys? They cleaned us out."

"They sure did." He lifted his chin. "Honestly, I wouldn't be surprised if there's a baby boom nine months from now."

"Well, thank you. Gardenia Flowers appreciates the business."

"Who?"

"Gardenia Flowers. That's the name of this place."

"Right," he said. "I think of it as Tina's Flowers. You're welcome. Now grab your purse. Do you prefer omelets, or waffles?"

"That's a weird question. I like both."

"Come on," he said. "Your sister said you could take the morning off and have breakfast with me." He leaned down and looked her dead in the eyes. "I know you don't have any flowers to sell, so don't try to bluff me."

"Never," she said.

"Now put a note on the door, and let's go get some breakfast. I haven't eaten at Delilah's yet, and I hear it's good."

Delilah's was more than just good.

"Okay," she said.

She quickly wrote up a sign for the door, apologizing for being sold out for the day, and locked up.

Luca started walking in the wrong direction.

"Delilah's is up this way," she said.

"I've got a lot to learn, Ms. Neighborhood Expert." He turned and caught up with her easily, thanks to his long strides.

The guy had to be six foot three, at least. Tina was not short, but she felt short next to him. Tina had done some modeling in her early teens. Nothing too fancy, just for local malls and catalogs. She'd thought she might have a career in modeling, but then she'd stopped growing. So, she went on to do what felt like the exact opposite of modeling, and got into wrestling.

Tina caught their reflection in the shop windows they passed. The two looked like they could be a couple. They matched, but without being too matchy-matchy, like those old married couples who bought the same ski jackets every season.

Luca was wearing his usual boots and jeans. Tina wore her favorite sandals, with leggings and a long tunic-style shirt. The shirt was teal, and she wore it with a green belt. She liked pairing colors that were tertiary on the color wheel, such as teal and chartreuse, or red and orange. Some people preferred complementary colors, the ones that were across the color wheel from each other, but Tina liked how tertiary colors vibrated with energy. It was what distinguished her floral arrangements from her sister's.

She was only thinking about her clothes because Luca kept looking over at her. His mouth kept moving, like he was forever on the verge of saying something about how she was dressed, but he stopped short of commenting.

What he couldn't have known was that ever since the day Luca had walked into Gardenia Flowers, Tina had stepped up her game with her appearance. Instead of throwing on shorts and whatever shirt wasn't wrinkled, she actually spent time picking out clothes. Just in case he came in. She'd been shaving her legs every day. And not just to the knees.

He grinned at her. "You must be thinking about something juicy," he said. "You've got mischief all over your face."

She rubbed her stomach. "Just thinking about waffles."

They arrived at Delilah's. The restaurant was impossible to miss, with its eight-foot-tall teapot perched high above the door. The building sat on the corner of the block and was a local landmark.

They walked in, and the waitress, Maggie, seated them in a big corner booth. Maggie gave Luca the stink eye but didn't say anything. The booths were normally reserved for larger parties, but the place was quiet, even for a Thursday morning. They'd gotten lucky with their timing. On the weekends, the brunch lineup circled the block.

"That's quite the teapot over the door," Luca said. "If I wasn't afraid of you teasing me, I might even say it's cute."

"It's one of the things Baker Street is famous for," she said. "Back when I was little, when Delilah still worked here, the teapot was flat and made out of plywood. It was getting worn out, and the city thought it was a hazard. One gust of wind, and it could have sailed down the street, causing an accident. It happened with the shoe repair shop, which is why they have the small sign now. Anyway, Delilah didn't want to get rid of it, so she got some kids from the art college to make her something as a school project. The base is steel, or pure iron, I think —"

"It's steel," he said.

"Good eye."

"I do know my alloys. Plus nothing is made of pure iron anymore." He gestured for her to go on.

"And the teapot itself is made from Styrofoam. They sanded it really smooth and coated it with a hardener. When you see it in person, you can see the flaws, but in photos, it looks like it's made of porcelain."

Maggie returned with tea for Tina, and coffee plus more stink eye for Luca. She took their order and left them again.

Since they were already talking about Styrofoam, Tina told Luca about her adventures trying to cut letters for a sign for the flower shop. It had been a failure.

"You can't cut the foam with a bread knife," Tina said. "I mean, you can, and that's what they recommend if you're using it in construction, but it doesn't give you a smooth, paintable edge. You have to use a hot wire and melt your way through, but nobody's hand is steady enough to cut it straight. Most of the commercial signs you see around town are cut by lasers."

Luca said, "You sure talk a lot about Styrofoam for a first date."

"Styrofoam is highly underrated," she said. "You can use it to make giant boulders that you can throw at people without killing them. Like my sister."

"Megan? She could definitely take a Styrofoam boulder or two."

"She'd probably enjoy it," Tina said, then, "You just called this a date, Luca. I thought this was supposed to be a networking meeting, for you to pump me for information about the locals."

"This definitely counts as a date. This is number one."

"Oh, we're counting. Interesting." She looked down and fiddled around with the tea bag in her teapot, which was a miniature version of the giant teapot over the entrance. Why was he counting dates?

"Number one," he repeated.

"If you say so," she said, then it hit her. She'd read about this on dating websites over the years. Date number four was supposedly the magic number. The date that your pants magically disappeared. Was Luca implying that he was only three dates away from getting into her pants? Pretty bold for a guy who kept asking her to make bouquets for other women.

"Your sister said you don't date very much," Luca said. He was speaking softly, but his voice was so deep and rich that it cut easily through her internal chatter.

"I don't."

"Your sister didn't say why."

"I've been on a few first dates, but not many second dates. Maybe I'm too old fashioned, calling them dates. My sister says I'm twenty-nine going on seventy. Do people even date anymore?"

"They do."

"But mostly, people do hookups. Or there's this gradual transition that you don't notice. One minute you're just friends, like in a group of friends, and then you're together."

"Is that how it works?" His sky-blue eyes were locked on her. His focus and presence were almost overwhelming. He wasn't just waiting for his next chance to talk. He was listening.

Tina's eyes burned, and her chest ached. She couldn't handle this. He was too intense. Why was she talking so much? Her voice was starting to remind her of Megan talking, blathering on and saying nothing. Just taking up attention.

"Luca, I really need to get back to the shop. What if..."

Just then, Maggie arrived with their food.

She gave Luca a stern look. "I hear you're the man who bought Ralph's Garage," she said. It was not a friendly conversational opener. More of an accusation.

He looked up and gave her a charming smile. "I am that man. We'll be reopening soon."

Maggie, who was fifty and had an impressive scowl, didn't smile back. "I've been taking my Honda to Ralph's since the day I bought it," she said. The edge in her voice said she was more than willing to give up her future tip in exchange for expressing her feelings in the present.

"I hope you'll keep bringing your Honda in," Luca said. "We'll have some service bays dedicated to bikes, but I do have a plan to retain all the loyal Ralph's Garage customers."

The scowl eased slightly. "Really?"

He turned up the sunshine on his grin. "It's my personal pledge," he said. He glanced at her name tag. "Maggie, I solemnly vow to keep you satisfied."

Maggie's face lost a decade's worth of scowl lines. She twirled a lock of dyed-auburn hair around her finger. "I like the sound of that." She turned to me. "You want more hot water, Tina?"

"Whenever you get a minute," I said.

"More coffee for me," Luca said.

Maggie patted him on the shoulder in a motherly way. "Your last cup was old. I'm surprised you got it down. But don't you worry, honey. I'll put on a fresh pot. Just for you."

After she left, Tina said to Luca, "That was impressive, Mr. Lowell. I bet you could charm the pants right off a pants salesman."

"I'll take that as a compliment. And thank you again for warning me about the locals. Your idea wasn't exactly new to me. I was on the fence about keeping a bay for servicing cars, but then you did your own magic, and you helped me make up my mind. A person could say that you talked my pants right off."

"And then you talked *my pants* off, and got me to play hookie from work to have breakfast with you."

"And now neither of us is wearing any pants at all."

Tina picked up her utensils and contemplated a plan of attack for her giant waffle.

"Who needs pants," she said.

"Pants just get in the way," he agreed.

"For our next date, pants are optional."

He murmured a wordless agreement.

"Not literally," she said. "That was just a joke."

He shrugged.

She blushed furiously and dug into her waffle.

As Tina ate, she gave herself another talking to. *Tina, do not think about pants-optional activities with Luca. Do not think about kissing him, or any of the jungle gym stuff. Calm down, girl. This is only date one.*

And besides, there's something very wrong with Luca that you haven't figured out. He's always sending women flowers to apologize. Take it slow, and figure out what's wrong with him before you even consider going pants-optional.

Luca's fork and knife squeaked on his plate. The white dish was nearly bare. His omelet and hash browns were gone.

Tina watched in awe as he inhaled a triangle-shaped piece of toast in two bites. The man ate food like he was loading coal into the furnace of a steam engine. The last guy she'd dated had been a vegan who didn't enjoy eating anything but candy. He'd been the one who'd gotten her hooked on fuzzy peaches. He'd given her his stash when he discovered that the brand he'd bought in bulk was made using gelatin, or, as he called it, hoof juices.

Luca caught Tina watching him. He slowed down the furnace-loading operation.

"I do have manners," he said. "I guess I forgot them back at the garage."

"Eating quickly must come in handy sometimes," she said. "It would fend off my sister, who's always taking food from me."

He held up his knife. "That's what this is for. Meal defense."

"Luckily, our mother helped us get past the stage of development where meals ended in stabbings."

"Sounds like a good woman." He pointed to the tray of miniature spreads. "Is that marmalade?"

She passed it over, then watched with amusement as he delicately spread marmalade on the remaining slices of toast.

She couldn't take her eyes off his hands. His finger didn't fit through the tiny handle on the coffee cup, so he held the cup loosely in one hand. The small white cup looked like a miniature kid's toy in his palm.

Tina longed to turn into a small white cup and disappear in those hands.

They made small talk for a while, about Delilah's, the weather, the neighborhood, the city. Luca didn't volunteer any personal details, and Tina didn't ask. Later, after the date, she would regret not asking about the women he'd bought bouquets for, but it wasn't on her mind that morning at breakfast. For once, she wasn't worrying about the future or living in the past. It was wonderful to be where she was, in the present, with Luca. Plus she had waffles.

Luca asked, "How long have you been working at the flower shop?"

"My mother bought the business when I was five. I've never worked anywhere else."

"College?"

"I've started a few different courses. Nothing finished."

"Starting things is easy. Finishing is tough."

"How about you? College?"

"This and that. Mostly I traveled around. Who wants to stick around in one place like a tree? We've got two legs for a reason. I did an apprenticeship in Australia for a year."

"You're the exact opposite of me. I've never left the country. My life must seem claustrophobic to you."

He studied her quietly for a moment.

She chewed some more of her food. She realized she was full, so she set down her utensils and pushed the plate away.

"What's Australia like?"

"I'll buy you a book," he said. "You don't want to hear me talk about some place you've never been."

"I might."

"They have kangaroos," he said. "Seriously, I'll get you a book."

"Sure."

"How are you liking this date?"

"I think it's going well."

"If I ask you to come to the paint store with me and help me pick out paint colors, will that count as date number two?"

"No. It would just be a continuation of this date, number one. Also, I really should be getting back to the shop. There's always paperwork to do, and phone orders. It will be good to catch up on a few things."

"All work and no play..."

She finished his line with "Is good for catching up on paperwork."

He nodded for Maggie to bring over the bill.

"In that case, I'll have to brave the paint store on my own." Dramatically, he added, "All by myself."

"I'm sure that a big, strong guy like you will be just fine."

"What if I have a paint color emergency? Who am I going to call?"

"You could put in a phone call to your local florist. I hear they're good with things like color."

"What if I have a paint color emergency when you're not at the shop? Would I have to deal with your sister and all of her sense of humor?"

"You could text me. On my personal number."

He whipped out his phone, typed something in, then handed it to her. "Fill this in for me, would you?"

She put in her number. He'd named her in his contacts as *Flower Shop Girl, Great Legs, Nice Smile, Kinda Bossy.*

She glanced up and saw that he was grinning. He'd meant for her to see that.

Did the games ever stop?

Chapter 8

Tina's best friend pulled a hot baking tray full of nacho chips from the oven. The chips were covered in melted cheese, ground beef, and bacon.

The girls were in Tina's little house, and Rory was wearing a hair net over her dark, curly hair. Rory worked in catering, so she always had hair nets in her pockets, and she always wore them. For Rory, seeing hair in food, even if she knew it was her own hair, made her sick.

The nacho chips had all slid to one side. The oven was a tiny European model, since a regular stove wouldn't have fit in the compact kitchen. Tina had never found baking trays that fit perfectly, so she'd kept using the ones she borrowed from the main house, propping up one side inside the oven with a small ceramic trivet. The trays would fit, if they were at a ten-degree angle.

Rory said, "This toy oven of yours is ridiculous."

"No. *You're* ridiculous," Tina said. That was one of their little games. Rory would make a comment about something, and Tina would turn it around to be about Rory. It was juvenile, but they'd been friends for so long.

It was Saturday afternoon, and Rory had come over to hang out until Luca came by at eight o'clock for a second date.

Ever since Tina gave Luca her phone number over breakfast at Delilah's, he'd been messaging her. First, it had been about paint colors. Then, about the merits of brushed silver cabinet handles versus polished brass. Eventually, he'd bargained that he'd stop bugging her about dinner on Friday—he was busy with the renovation, anyway—if she'd let him take her to a movie on Saturday.

As soon as he made the offer, Tina had frozen up. It was one thing to goof around with Luca in person, in the moment, but this was a formal invitation. Or as formal as things got in the era of smartphones. It was a clear and direct question, for which there could only be a yes or a no answer. It was like being asked to prom. It was a big deal.

She said no and made up a fake excuse. She even convinced herself that she did need to be home Saturday night, using her new rake to remove moss from the lawn before it took over.

But then Rory found out, and Rory turned on the waterworks again. She was even more dramatic than she'd been in the car on the way home from the spa weekend. Rory had sniffed her way through a long, complicated speech about how her own phobias were hurting others, and that she was an anchor on Tina's life. She'd used the word *anchor* multiple times, along with other boat and sailing metaphors.

Tina suspected the tears were fake, since the speech about sailors and sirens was a little too polished, but Tina had eventually given in to Rory's wishes.

It was just a movie, after all. As far as second dates went, it would be an easy one. How hard could it be to sit in the dark with someone in a public place, not talking, just eating candies and popcorn?

Rory removed the hair net, stood as far back from the nachos as she could inside the tiny house, and shook out her curly dark hair. Her solitary white streak peeked through. Rory's hair was a few shades darker than Tina's, except for one streak of white near the temples. She used to dye the streak dark, just so people wouldn't ask if she had paint in her hair and try to touch it. Lately, she'd been letting it grow out.

Rory kept looking over at the clock that sat on Tina's fireplace mantel, in her shrine of photos. Rory didn't usually check the time so much. Just like how she knew everyone else's schedules, she seemed to always know exactly what time it was.

She had to have been nervous about Luca coming over. When Tina had agreed to the date, Rory had promised to stick around so she could meet Luca. However, judging by her furtive glances at the clock, Tina knew it was more likely Rory would freak out and run off before he arrived.

"Relax," Tina said.

"Since when did saying that word ever help anyone relax?"

"You're right. Feel free to stress out as much as you'd like."

"How long is the movie going to take?" Rory checked the clock again.

"Aren't they usually around two hours, give or take?"

"Is it a nine o'clock showing? That should get you home by eleven-thirty."

"I didn't know I had a curfew."

"You don't. But you have to let me know the minute you get in. I won't be able to sleep or do anything until I know you're back home, safe and sound."

"Would it make you feel any better if I promised you that under no circumstances will I let him touch my undergarments?"

Rory bristled visibly at the mention of undergarments. Tina hadn't said any of the no-no words, such as *panties* or *bra*, but the abstract idea alone was enough to bother Rory.

The girls took their seats at the round table overlooking the backyard and started eating cheesy nachos from the lopsided tray. Secretly, Tina actually liked how the nachos came out when baked at a ten-degree angle. One side was dry and crunchy, and the other side was extra gooey. You could go back and forth, varying the texture.

After a moment, Rory spoke what must have been on her mind. "Promise me you won't move to Australia with him."

"What? Australia?"

They both looked over at the big coffee table book Luca had dropped off at the flower shop on Friday. It was a collection of photos showing the diversity of Australia. He said it was the book he'd promised to give her over breakfast at Delilah's, but Tina had a feeling he'd been stopping in to make sure she didn't wriggle out of their date plans for the next day.

"He just bought a garage on Baker Street," Tina assured her best friend. "He's not even open yet. They're still renovating. He's not going to Australia. He's not going anywhere. And neither am I."

"There's something wrong with him. I have a bad feeling."

"You always have a bad feeling."

Rory narrowed her eyes at her best friend. "He must be really good looking. I bet he gives you a *party* feeling in your you-know-what."

"Rory! Was that a vague reference to sexual desire?"

She frowned. "Shut up."

"A *party feeling*? Really?"

She clapped both hands over her ears. "Forget I said that! Never say that word again!"

"I can't say party? What if there's a birthday party I need to invite you to?"

"You know what I mean," she growled.

They crunched more cheesy nachos. She looked at the clock on the mantel. It was coming up on seven-thirty.

"Stop looking at the time," Tina said. "You're making me nervous."

"Stop eating so loud," Rory said. "I can hear the food in your mouth."

"I'm eating normally, like a normal person. I'm not loud. Meenie is the loud eater."

"You could eat more quietly if you wanted to."

Tina slowed down her chewing. In addition to her quirks about certain words, Rory had misophonia. She didn't hate all sounds, but if she was agitated, anything could set her off.

Rory looked at the clock five more times.

Tina kept thinking about what Rory had said, and about how she was feeling in her body. She *did* get warm whenever she thought about Luca. If she happened to be hungry, or her feet hurt, thinking about him made the discomfort go away. But then, when she was around him in person, there was another layer to it. Lots of layers.

As Tina watched her best friend eat and watch the clock, she wondered if Rory had any way of understanding how Luca made her feel.

Finally, she asked, "Rory, do *you* ever get a party feeling?"

Rory jerked her head up, her eyes wide and horrified.

Tina said, "Maybe for a cute singer, or a movie actor? Not for anyone we know in person, of course."

Rory's face went gray.

For a moment, Tina thought Rory was going to throw up. Instead, Rory stood, grabbed her bag, and quietly let herself out the door without a word.

"Sorry I asked," Tina said to the closed door, but the truth was, she wasn't sorry. If Rory was going to push Tina to do things that made her uncomfortable, Tina was going to do the same to her. Fair was fair.

Tina finished eating, brushed her teeth, and fussed around with her hair. Curly hair always had an attitude. The only time it curled perfectly was in the morning on the day she had a haircut booked.

The intercom connected to the main house buzzed. Tina groaned. She knew exactly what was happening. Luca had ignored her directions, just like every pizza delivery guy did. He'd gone to the main house instead of coming around the back to her tiny house.

She grabbed her purse and ran out to intercept him before Meenie could get to him.

Too late.

He stood on the front step of the main house, talking to Tina's sister. They were laughing about their shared adventure, when they'd sold out the flower shop on Wednesday to his contractors.

"Oh, there'll be a baby boom in nine months," she said. "Guaranteed. I hope you've got your shop renovated by then, because your guys won't be getting any sleep with all those babies around."

"We'll be open long before the baby boom," he said. "It's all on track."

"Hey," Tina said, announcing her presence.

Luca turned slowly. The setting sunlight caught his wavy brown hair, turning it golden.

"There's our Teenie," he said. "Thanks, Meenie. See you around." He gave her a nod goodbye.

Megan stayed on the porch.

Tina made the shoo gesture at her sister.

Megan gave Tina a dirty look then turned and went into the house.

"You didn't read my directions," Tina said to Luca. "You're as bad as all the pizza delivery guys in this city."

"I read your directions. You live in the tiny house in the backyard."

"You read them and chose to ignore them?"

"If you'll note the time, it's not eight o'clock yet." He tilted his head to the side. "Are you always this tough on guys? No wonder they don't ask you for second dates."

She snorted.

He held out his arms and asked, "What do you think? Do I clean up good?" He wore a button-down shirt with dress slacks and stylish leather shoes.

"I like you better in the motorbike boots," she said.

He nodded. "So that's how it is. You like the bad boy image. Good to know."

"I like it when people are themselves."

He pointed at her outfit, which was a flower-print sundress, topped in a cardigan.

"That explains why you brought the flower shop with you, Flower Shop Girl."

She frowned at her dress, which suddenly seemed way too floral and mature.

"I don't know why I'm wearing this," she said. "My best friend didn't like it, either."

"That was meant to be a compliment," he said. "You look pretty. Over the last few weeks, I've developed an appreciation of flowers. Did you know there are flowers everywhere? Even dandelions are kinda cool, if you look at them closely."

"Dandelions are not cool," she said, crossing her arms playfully. "Not cool at all, Luca."

He chuckled.

They were still standing on the front step, and Tina sensed her sister nearby. Megan was probably listening through the door, like the nosy brat she was.

"We should get going so we don't miss the previews," Tina said. "What movie are we going to see?"

"It's a surprise." He offered her his elbow in an old-fashioned sort of way.

She tucked her hand into the crook of his arm and walked with him to the sidewalk.

Parked directly in front of the house was an old-fashioned-looking motorbike. He handed her a helmet.

A bike. She should have known.

"I'm not dressed for this," she said, backing away. "Sorry."

"Then go back to your place and throw on something else," he said. "You're not getting out of this that easy."

"I wasn't trying to get out of anything."

"Good," he said. "Get changed into something else. I'll be here."

"What should I wear?"

"Ideally, leather pants." He grinned. "Tight ones."

She put her hand on her hip. "Do I look like the kind of girl who can pull off tight leather pants?"

He raised an eyebrow. "Yes. A thousand percent. Yes."

The front door of the main house suddenly opened. Tina's sister yelled out excitedly, "I have some leather pants you can borrow, Teenie."

Luca held up one hand. "There you go."

Tina shook her head. "I knew she was listening."

"At least she's helpful," Luca said.

Tina gave Megan a dirty look. "So helpful," she said.

Chapter 9

Tina Gardenia was nervous to get on a motorbike for the first time in her life. Almost as nervous as she was about being seen in the leather pants she was wearing. They were so tight. They left nothing to the imagination.

Luca watched her as she fussed with her hair, then tried to pull on the helmet. She barely got it on the top of her head before giving up.

"It's too small," she said. "Either this helmet's too small, or my head's too big."

He got closer and used his big hands to measure the circumference of her skull. She liked the feeling of his fingers wrapping around her head. It was a nice way to be measured and assessed. Comforting. It reminded her of her visits to the pediatrician when she'd been growing up. The doctor was a kindly older man, always quick to laugh. He'd squeeze her arm or shoulder, then pronounce her to be growing up tall and strong, like a sturdy weed. Then he'd say he was proud of her. She hadn't done anything in particular since the previous visit besides get older, but when he paid her the compliment, it always made her feel so proud, and excited about the future. Tina had almost forgotten about that good feeling.

Luca lifted his hands away slowly then studied the circle he'd made. "Your head is not big," he said. "Helmets have to fit tight. It's a safety feature. It's going to feel tight for a minute, but as soon as you get it past your ears, you'll be fine. You're not claustrophobic, are you?"

"Not that I know of. And if you saw the size of the house I live in, you wouldn't ask that." The house couldn't be seen from the front yard, so he hadn't seen it yet.

"Try again with the helmet," he said. "You've already got your leather pants and your leather jacket. You look ready to rumble. Stop stalling, Flower Shop Girl."

She took a deep breath and jammed her head all the way into the helmet. He was right about it getting easier once she got it past her ears.

He helped her fasten the helmet's buckle under her chin, his hands enveloping hers.

He pulled on his own helmet, turned, and threw one long, muscled leg over the leather seat of the bike.

Without any delay, Tina hopped up behind him. She felt safe in her helmet, and she felt brave in her leather pants. She put her arms around Luca's waist, and she felt even safer and braver.

He started the bike's engine, and the night air filled with a deep rumble. The vibration in the seat was surprising. She felt it through her whole body.

Then the whole world moved, blurring alongside them. Luca adjusted her hands like they were Velcro straps, pulling them apart and then back together so she was hugging him even tighter.

They rode along streets Tina had traveled a thousand times. Familiar territory. Everything was slightly different on a motorbike. The trees had more color. Everything was denser, closer together. People turned their heads and looked her way. People didn't do that when you were in a car.

They continued on past the local movie theater. "You missed a turn," she said to the back of Luca's black helmet. "The movie theater's back behind us."

He must not have heard her over the rumble. She'd barely heard herself.

They kept riding.

Eventually, they pulled off the main road and turned into another residential neighborhood. They pulled up behind a giant white trailer, and he parked the bike.

Tina's legs were shaking when she stepped off the bike. The leather pants felt like they were the only things holding her up. The engine was off, but she could still feel the rumbling in her body, especially the center of her chest.

They were surrounded by big trailers, a catering truck, and filming equipment.

She looked around. "This is the movie?" Her voice was muffled by the helmet.

"This is the movie," he said through his helmet. "Oh. Did you think I meant a finished movie?"

"Uh. Yeah. Smarty pants."

They both took off their helmets. Luca ruffled his hands through his wavy brown hair. It was impossible for her to look away. No wonder girls fell for guys who rode bikes. That ruffling of the hair was really something.

Two people with clipboards and headsets rushed past them.

Tina asked Luca, "Are we allowed to be here?"

The people with the clipboards were telling a lady walking her dog that the whole block was a closed set.

"Don't worry, Flower Shop Girl," he said. "We're officially invited."

"How'd you swing that? Hollywood connections?"

"I'm renting them some bikes from my private collection. The director told me to come by tonight and watch. They're shooting an outdoor scene that should be pretty entertaining. It's a romantic comedy. That guy everyone loves is in it. Dalton Deangelo."

"But it's just one scene," she said. "Not a full movie."

"We don't have to stay long if you're not having fun." He thumbed over his shoulder. "We can still hit the local multiplex. I had a look at the marquee, and we've got our choice of superheroes or... other superheroes."

She rubbed her hands on her leather pants. "I might be overdressed for the multiplex."

"True. One look at you, and nobody will pay attention to the screen."

She felt her cheeks flush. "I mean, I probably look like one of those geeks who dress up like superheroes to go see a movie."

He held very still, studying her. "What do you want, Tina?"

She was genuinely stumped by the question.

He went on. "Do you want me to talk you into going to the movie theater and pretending we're geeks?"

She didn't like what he was saying about talking her into things, not to mention his tone. "No," she said sullenly.

"Good," he said. "Then we'll go ahead with the date as planned. You can plan the next one."

She didn't like the sound of that, either, but said nothing.

"Come on." He took her hand in his. She did like that. "Let's go watch some of the movie happening on this block."

He led the way toward the action, both of them stepping over thick cables criss-crossing the ground.

Luca talked to the two people with the clipboards and headsets, and they set up a pair of folding chairs for the movie attendees, right near the action.

Luca and Tina watched as the crew set up a shot, taking a hundred measurements and notes. Finally, a bell rang. They were filming.

The scene was of a guy picking up a girl at her house for a date. At the end of the scene, they drove away on a motorbike very similar to the one Luca had brought Tina there on.

At the end of the scene, Luca turned to Tina, his blue eyes looking pale gray in the artificial light. "I was really hoping for a kiss."

She leaned over and kissed him, right on the lips.

He pulled away, looking surprised. "I meant in the shot they're filming. It's supposed to be a romantic comedy. There's kissing in those, right?"

She covered her mouth with her fingertips, mortified.

He grinned. "If I'd known getting a kiss from you was so easy, I would have asked sooner."

"Oh, Luca." She shook her head, still so embarrassed.

One of the PAs with a headset approached them with takeout cups. There was one coffee and one tea. The tea was Tina's favorite, the same one she'd had at Delilah's. It was a special blend, not the sort of thing you'd expect to find at an on-set catering truck. Tina could tell by the way Luca was looking at her that getting her favorite tea had been no accident.

After the PA walked away, Luca took the tea from her hands and set it down on the ground, on the other side of his chair.

He slid toward her on his chair, so his hips and legs were in contact with hers.

"Body heat," he explained. "Just so you don't get cold when there's no action going on. It can take a long time in between takes."

"These leather pants are actually pretty warm. I'm glad I didn't stick with the dress."

"I almost wish you had. As hot as you look in those leather pants, if you were colder, you might be talked into sitting on my lap."

"You actually think you're that much of a salesman?"

"I *know* I'm that much of a salesman." He gave her an eyebrow waggle then wrapped one long arm around her shoulders. He wasn't wearing a jacket, so the heat of his arm came through his long-sleeved dress shirt. She felt his warmth, even through her leather jacket. He was like a furnace.

On the set, the crew members were taking more measurements and making lighting changes. The two actors—one of them was the dreamy Dalton Deangelo—had retreated to their trailers.

Tina turned to Luca, preparing to ask him how many bikes he had. Before she could speak, he reached up and softly stroked her jaw.

She pulled back. "What are you doing?"

"There must have been some dirt on the inside of your helmet," he said. "Don't move." He licked his thumb then used it to clean the side of her face. "Much better," he pronounced.

"You put your spit on my face," she said.

"You started it," he said. "Remember when you kissed me?"

"That was barely a peck. There was no tongue. My mouth left your mouth exactly as it had been."

He paused and gave her a look she would later describe as *smoldering*. "My mouth will never be the same," he said gravely.

"A big, tough guy like you? Being changed forever by one little kiss?"

"Big, tough guys have feelings, too."

"So you keep telling me."

"I'm hoping for another kiss," he said.

She waved at the set. "Be patient," she said. "I heard someone talking about a rewrite on the scene to turn up the heat."

"I didn't mean on the set."

She shrugged. "I don't know what to say. That's probably your best bet, if you want any more kissing action tonight."

He rubbed his chin and gave her a thoughtful look. "Did your best friend make you promise you wouldn't kiss me? What's her name? Rory?"

"How do you know about Rory?" She immediately realized the answer to the question. "I'm going to kill my sister," she said. "Did she tell you everything?"

"She told me enough. I've known people like Rory." Luca looked down at her leather pants then back up to her eyes. "What do you think her issue is?"

"Where do we even start? She's got a lot of issues."

"But the main root of the problem," he said. "Why is she so guarded?"

"It's pretty obvious. People have hurt her in the past."

"But everyone's been hurt," he said. "Not everyone shuts down. Not everyone gets stuck in arrested development. Most people move on with their lives."

She held out her hands. "Beats me. I don't know the self-help lingo. That's more my sister's thing."

"Did you move from the main house directly into the tiny house in the backyard?"

She gave him a steady look. Slowly, she said, "Yesss?" She sensed a direction to his line of questioning.

"And you've never worked anywhere but the flower shop?"

She crossed her arms. "Just because I didn't spend my early twenties traveling all over the world with a backpack and getting bitten by fleas in hostels doesn't mean I haven't had life experiences."

"You sound defensive."

"Just telling the truth. Would you rather I lie to you?"

He leaned back. After a long moment, he asked, "How did you know about the fleas?"

"Everyone knows hostels are full of fleas."

He gave her another long look. "There are a lot of layers to your onion, Flower Shop Girl."

"Isn't that what second dates are all about?" She added, "Bad Boy Biker Boy."

He grinned. "Bad Boy Biker Boy? I like it. When the garage opens, I'll have to get that engraved on my office door."

"What it needs to say is Mr. Boss Man Bad Boy Biker Boy."

He tilted his head to the side. "I'm a Boss Man but also a Biker Boy? Which is it? Am I a man or a boy?"

"I don't know."

He grabbed the drink containers from the sidewalk and handed her one of them.

She took a sip and nearly spat it out. "Luca, I think I'm drinking your coffee. Blech."

"You got your spit on the rim."

She rubbed it off. "You'll be fine." They traded cups.

"I'm glad you noticed," he said. "I thought the coffee was just really weak."

"And I thought they brewed my tea using a goat's backside."

He chuckled. "You're not a coffee fan."

"Not of *that* coffee." She looked around. "I wonder where they keep the goats."

He took a sip and looked thoughtful. "I can't tell if it's good coffee or not. All I can taste is your lips."

"I'm sure the feeling will pass."

He gazed down at her mouth. "I don't want it to."

She suddenly became aware of all the people around them. Several were looking their way. The workers must have been bored with the slow setup between filming takes, and happy to watch her and Luca for entertainment.

She edged away from him and zipped up her jacket. "Look," she said, waving at the brightly lit patch of street. "They're doing something with the set. Someone's up in that tree, cutting away branches. That must be what's taking so long."

"For someone who wasn't sure about hanging out on a film set, you sure seem interested now." He gazed at her steadily. "Or are you just changing the subject away from your lips, and how they taste on my lips?"

"The film set is interesting."

"Is anything else interesting?" He reached over and placed one large hand on her thigh before giving it a squeeze.

"I'm not bored."

"Only boring people get bored," he said.

"Then I guess I'm pretty boring, because I get bored a lot. Working at a flower shop has its moments, but it's not exactly a thrill ride."

He squeezed her leg. "What about me? Am I a thrill ride?"

"Your old bike is kinda neat. I guess you could say that the whole package"—she waved to encompass both him and the bike, parked down the street—"is a thrill ride."

His hand was hot and heavy on her leg. "That's all the encouragement I need," he said, then he turned to watch the film crew on the set while he sipped his coffee.

* * *

After two hours of flirting and watching the filming, Luca hopped on his bike, and Tina hopped on behind him. The helmet had gone on much easier that time.

She held on tightly, savoring the feeling of Luca wrapped in her arms. She didn't want the ride to end, but it did.

When they got to her place, she deliberately led him up to the main house instead of her own. He fell a few paces behind, and when she turned around, she caught him staring at her butt.

"Those leather pants," he said. "I thought you were a scooter girl when I met you, but it turns out I was wrong."

She put her hand on her hip. "Am I a biker chick now? Is that all it takes? A pair of leather pants and two rides on your bike?"

He looked at his bike then back at her. "Was that your first time? Why didn't you tell me?"

"Couldn't you tell by the death grip I used to hang on to you? I'm surprised you didn't pass out from lack of oxygen and crash us into a telephone pole."

He stepped in closer and looked down into her eyes. "You can hang on to me as tight as you want. I can take it."

She took a step back, away from the intensity he was giving her. "Luca, I had a wonderful time, but I'm not going to invite you in."

He looked up to the second-floor window. "I wouldn't want to go in anyway. Your sister's watching us from the window. She's probably dying to interrogate you."

Tina turned and shooed Megan away from the window. She didn't budge.

"Sorry about you-know-who," Tina said. "She's probably making popcorn for the second half."

"There's a second half?"

"Sort of." She stood up on her toes and quickly kissed him. Again. He was surprised. Again. She pulled away before he could kiss her back. Just how she wanted it.

"Thanks for the movie date," she said, reaching for the door.

"Can we do it again some time?"

"I don't know, Luca. We already saw them shoot that scene twenty-seven times. I'm sure your director buddy is really talented, and Dalton Deangelo doesn't hurt the eyes, but I don't think I could sit through it again."

"I meant something else."

"If you're asking me if we can do something else sometime, the answer is maybe."

She yanked open the door and ran inside before he could talk her into anything more specific.

Chapter 10

Something else turned out to be dinner. *Sometime* turned out to be Wednesday.

Luca Lowell took Tina Gardenia out for dinner at a restaurant in the area. It had just reopened under new owners.

Tina felt like the prettiest girl in the world when they walked in. She noticed she always felt that way whenever she was holding Luca's arm. His glow was contagious.

It was their third date, and he kept dropping that fact into conversation.

She asked, feigning forgetfulness, "Is this really the third one already?"

"And the best one yet." He yawned and rubbed his eyes. "Sorry about that. You're not boring, I swear. It's this place. It's too dark."

"They must be going for an intimate ambiance." She looked up at the chandeliers, which were high above them, and filled with low-lumen bulbs. "The new owners changed a lot. You'd never guess this was once a Chunky Cheese."

"Did you say Chuck E. Cheese?"

"*Chunky* Cheese," she said. "It was a family-oriented pizza place with a rat mascot. Or was it a hedgehog?"

"You really know this neighborhood."

"That's what you get for sticking around and committing to one place for almost thirty years."

He yawned again then apologized.

"Don't worry about it," she said. "I'll take it as a compliment that you feel relaxed around me."

He smiled, his face looking weary. "I barely slept last night. Maybe two hours. Anyone who said renovations are easy is a liar."

"Nobody says that."

"My contractor did."

"Your contractor is a liar."

"I'm starting to realize that."

She squinted at the menu. The items were written in blue text on a black background. "The menu at Chunky Cheese was a lot easier to read," she said.

"Did you try every item on the menu?"

"That sounds like something you'd do, Mr. Adventure. I got the four-cheese pizza, every time. Oh, except once I shared the vegan pizza with someone, just to see what it was about. Big mistake."

"You don't like soy cheese?"

"The cheese was the least of that pizza's problems. The sauce wasn't even tomato. It was orange. I think it was yams, maybe? Or carrots?"

"I can see why they went out of business."

"That wasn't it. Chunky Cheese was always busy, right until the end. But then Fred and Tannis, the owners, won the lottery. The actual lottery. They immediately packed up and moved down south. They're in a condo, and they've taken up golfing. They sent me a postcard last month."

"You really know everyone in this neighborhood, don't you?"

"You meet a few people over thirty years in the same spot." She squinted at the dark menu and tried to figure out what to order. When she looked up, Luca was yawning again.

She asked, "How late were you at the garage last night?"

"Not too long. Mostly, I spent the night lying awake in bed, unable to shut my brain off. One of my contractors has an alcohol abuse problem. By which I mean he drinks on the job and abuses my brand-new walls. I had to let him go."

"Yikes."

"Now we're running behind, and I've got a bunch of drywall holes to patch up."

"Is there anything I can help you with?"

"Good one. I bet you don't even know what side of a hammer is for hitting the nail."

She batted her eyelashes. "What's a hammer?"

He'd been starting to yawn again, but it turned into a laugh.

They ordered their dinner and ate. Luca perked up and stopped yawning once he had some food in his system. He'd been so tired and stressed that he'd forgotten to eat all day.

The food was good. Not as good as Chunky Cheese, but Tina predicted the new restaurant might last as long as two to three years.

The waiter came by to clear their dinner plates. His name was Edward, and he'd been working at that location for years. Back when it had been Chunky Cheese, he used to dress up in the rodent costume.

"May I interest you in dessert?" Edward asked.

Tina declined dessert—she'd eaten a bag of candy at work already—and asked, "Edward, what was that costume you used to dress up in? Was Chunky Cheese a rat or a hedgehog?"

"Definitely not a rat." He gave them both a theatrical double wink. "That would have been a trademark infringement." He waggled his eyebrows. "I like to think of Chunky as a guinea pig." He crossed his chest. "May he rest in peace." He leaned down and whispered, "We buried the costume in the old graveyard."

"I'm sure it was a very dignified service," Tina said.

Edward rubbed his hands together. "No dessert, then. Can I get you two some hot beverages?"

"Let's start with a triple espresso for me," Luca said. "The lady will have tea."

Tina waved both hands at the waiter. "Cancel that. No triple espresso." She gave Luca a serious look. "You'll never sleep tonight if you have a triple espresso now."

The waiter looked at me, then Luca, and said to him, "Tina is right. No caffeine after noon."

Luca frowned at both of them. "I thought the customer was always right," he said. To me, he said, "Is there anywhere I can take you where you don't know all the staff, and I can get what I want?"

Tina held up both hands. "Edward, you heard the man. Triple espresso. This is Luca Lowell, by the way. He's the new owner of Ralph's Garage."

Edward gave Luca a wary look. "Oh, I know who he is," he said cattily. "Where am I supposed to take my Toyota when it makes the squeaky sounds?"

"Bring it to me," Luca said, and he repeated the same speech he'd given at Delilah's. Edward seemed satisfied by the response.

After the waiter left, I said to Luca, "Sorry about trying to cancel your coffee order. We're only on our third date, and already I'm acting like a nagging old wife."

"I didn't really mind," he said. "What's that saying? Nagging is caring?"

"I don't think that's a saying."

He reached across the table and touched her hand. "Either way, it feels good to have someone looking out for me. It's been a long time since somebody cared."

The look of adoration on his face made her chest ache and her eyes burn.

But then he yawned again, and she got a different feeling. Not a good one. Luca was so big and tough, but seeing him tired and vulnerable like that made her uncomfortable. He was never tired or yawning in any of her daydreams. He was always larger than life in her mind. Nothing in the world was supposed to get through his thick skin and make him sick, or take him away.

"It's getting late," she said. "I'll catch a bus home so you can go straight home and get to bed. If I run out now, I can catch one without having to wait."

"But—"

"Not another word, Mr. Ten Yawns." She reached for her purse.

The waiter returned with the espresso, but she was already standing, clearly leaving.

Edward asked, "Is everything okay?"

Tina pointed at Luca. In her most naggy voice, she said, "Edward, don't you dare serve him any more coffee after this one. He needs to go home and get some sleep."

Edward gave her a knowing, happy look. "Okay," he said. "You're the boss."

Luca beamed, then he raised his eyebrows at Tina while pointing to his lips.

She walked around the table quickly, and leaned down before he could stand. She pecked him on the mouth.

He had been expecting it and looped his long arm around her waist. He kept her there just long enough for the kiss to register and for him to kiss her back. But he didn't hold her long enough for it to be too pushy. And, Tina had to admit to herself, the kiss had been better that way.

She was still buzzy when she hopped on the bus a few minutes later.

As soon as she sat down, though, everything shifted. There was a young couple, teenagers, making out in a back seat. Tina remembered other times she'd been on that same bus. With other people, under other circumstances.

Everything that had been positive about the evening reversed, like a magnet flipping polarity.

She couldn't get back home fast enough.

Once she was inside her cottage and alone again, she closed all the windows and blinds.

There was something she had to do. She hadn't done it in a while, and she was overdue. Her life had become unbalanced, and this was what she needed to make things feel steady and familiar again.

She pulled the shoe box from the top of the closet and prepared for the ritual. It wasn't a magic type of ritual, like a Wiccan thing—at least not that she knew of—just something that had helped her get through some hard times. She wiped down the table, dimmed the lights, and took a seat.

She opened the box and laid out the items, one at a time, beginning with the dried rose.

The blue dye that had been used to turn the white rose blue had faded away to a muddy gray. The dried petals were loose and threatened to disintegrate every time she handled it.

The flower would be nothing but garbage to anyone else who saw it, but it was the most precious thing she owned because it was a physical link. A lasting remnant from a time she'd loved someone with everything she had, and he'd loved her. Like Luca, he had been strong, too. Not big, but strong. Until he wasn't.

Once upon a time, she'd had everything, but then death had taken it all away.

Chapter 11

Prom – Ten Years Ago

Tina Gardenia's first love gave her a blue rose. He tried pinning it to her prom dress, but his hands were shaking. The photographer teased him about being nervous.

As he tried again to pin the corsage to Tina's dress, he hammed it up, making jokes about getting to first base by accident.

Looking into her eyes, he said, "Tina Gardenia, you'll make someone a beautiful bride someday."

"I shouldn't have picked this stupid dress," she said. "Everyone else looks amazing, and I look like some sort of deranged runaway bride."

"You look perfect. I wouldn't change a thing."

He kissed her, and they posed for their official prom photo.

The whole night, girls kept coming up to admire Tina's dress. The strapless gown was pale blue but looked white under the lighting in the gym. She did resemble a bride, "but in a good way," the other girls kept saying.

"This dress is so wrong," Tina kept saying. "I wish I could do everything all over again."

Every time Tina said it, her first love would simply say, "I wouldn't change a thing."

He died two months after graduation, and part of her died with him. Her friends who'd gone through breakups said they understood completely.

They couldn't have.

Her friends promised she'd get over it. She'd get over him.

She didn't.

Years passed, and then a decade. The picture of the couple at prom was still prominently displayed on Tina's fireplace mantel. Friends her age were updating their fireplaces with wedding photos and baby portraits. Tina couldn't imagine doing that.

What did that even mean, to *get over* something?

Did it mean that one day she could sell a prom corsage to a nervous young man in a tuxedo, and not burst into tears?

Chapter 12

The Present

Rory showed up at Tina's place on Saturday afternoon, lugging enough food to cater a party of ten.

"This is way too much," Tina said. "I'm only cooking dinner for myself and Luca."

"You?" Rory blinked at Tina. "*You're* cooking dinner?"

"Okay, fine. You're cooking dinner. But, just so you know, Luca's a big guy, but he's not *that* big. I've seen him put away food quickly, but nothing like this. You could feed a small army with all of this."

"So what? Use the leftovers to make sandwiches." She reached into a canvas bag and pulled out what appeared to be half a cow.

"Sandwiches? Sure. I'll just use up those ten loaves of bread I always keep in the house."

"Don't worry about bread," she said. "I brought bread."

She had. A whole bag's worth.

Tina helped Rory unload the groceries, keeping an eye on the giant half-cow in case it tried to make a getaway.

The miniature kitchen had very little counter space, so the girls hauled the dining table closer to fashion a prep area.

"What's all this crunchy dust?" Rory asked, scowling at the table surface.

"Housekeeper's day off," Tina joked, grabbing a cloth to give it a quick wipe.

The crunchy dust was from one of the dried rose petals. After taking everything out on Wednesday night, she'd gone to bed exhausted without cleaning up. She'd left everything out, right up until an hour before Rory had shown up. Unfortunately, the sun streaming in the window had degraded the rose further, causing more petals to fall off. She'd have to be more careful next time.

Rory said, "I have something to tell you."

"Oh?" Tina got out the cutting board and started chopping carrots.

Rory whispered something so softly, Tina couldn't hear it. Rory was trying, though. Her face was red with effort. What was she up to?

She whispered the word again, and this time Tina heard it. "Pantyhose."

"Rory!"

She said it again, louder. "Pantyhose."

"That's great, Rory! You're making so much progress. Is this from the hypnosis tapes?"

She shook her head. "Not the hypnosis tapes."

"Did my sister drag you to her loser support group?"

Rory shook her head again, but she was grinning, proud of her accomplishment.

Tina asked, "Can you say any of the other no-no words? Other types of underwear?"

Rory's grin faded. "No."

"That's still really good, Rory. I'd hug you right now, if it wouldn't send you screaming for the hills."

Rory gave Tina a serious look. "I'm still not normal. I'll never be normal." She grabbed some herbs and tossed them onto the cutting board. "Now get to work, or date number four will be the one where you serve raw meat and carrot sticks."

"Yes, Captain."

For the next hour, they chopped, and seared, and basted.

Rory worked for a caterer, so making a gourmet meal was well within her skills. Not Tina's. Tina must have been out of her mind when she'd offered to make Luca dinner.

Tina had been thinking a lot about date number four, and what was expected to happen—according to some advice websites—on the fourth date. The particular thing that, if it were to happen, would happen in her tiny house, on her fold-out sofa bed. That was assuming she still remembered *how* it was done. Was it like riding a bicycle? Did it all come back to you by sense memory?

Rory was chopping away, oblivious to Tina's nervous glances at the sofa-bed and the thoughts in her head. Tina wished she could talk to her best friend about how she was feeling, but Rory could barely say the word *pantyhose*. She wouldn't be able to handle any discussion of sex.

A terrible thought occurred to Tina. What if Luca was terrible at sex? Even worse than her? What if that was the reason he kept sending women flowers? What if he did some horrible, taboo thing that made women never want to see him again?

Rory stood up from checking the roast in the oven and looked at Tina. "Are you nervous? You look like you're going to throw up."

"It's our fourth date," Tina said. "That's the date where people traditionally…" She let the implication hang in the air.

Rory frowned. "Traditionally what?"

"You know," Tina said.

"I do not know."

Since Rory had made some progress, Tina decided to take a risk with a euphemism.

"Rory, the fourth date is when some people say a couple should... play Scrabble."

"Oh." Rory's cheeks got pink, and she started breathing in her upper chest, but she didn't run for the door. "But not Scrabble-Scrabble. You mean the other thing."

"Exactly."

Rory took a few more short breaths but still didn't run. "Okay. Date four. Scrabble time. Do you want that to happen?"

"Yes," Tina said without hesitation, surprising herself.

"Because he makes you feel..." Rory closed her eyes and grimaced.

"Party feelings," Tina said.

Rory clenched her fists, then released them, staying where she was. "I can handle this," she said to herself, then, "You can handle this. You've played Scrabble before."

"You know I have. You know everything about me. You know that—"

Rory held up one hand. "Not in technicolor detail, thank you."

Tina fanned her face. The small house was heating up, thanks to the giant roast in the tiny oven. "I appreciate you letting me talk about it," she said. "Maybe Meenie is right about therapy stuff. Maybe talking about your crap actually does help sort everything out."

"So, you're nervous about tonight," Rory said. "But not about the dinner. About the other thing. Which you want to do. So, what's the problem? You're not *me*. You'll be fine."

"There's lots to worry about," Tina said. "What if he's terrible at Scrabble? Like he puts the words in the wrong places, or he goes right for the triple word score immediately, instead of starting in the middle."

Rory's face froze.

Tina feared she'd broken her friend with the metaphor, but Rory gradually got her face muscles working again. "Okay," Rory said slowly. "Let's talk this out."

"Really? Wow. I'm so proud of you. And grateful, of course. The only other person I can talk to is my sister, and you know how she can be."

"Oh, I know." Rory grabbed the bottle of wine they'd been using for the sauce, and poured a glass for each of them. Rory didn't drink much, because of her family history, but she would have a glass on occasion.

They took the glasses over to the couch and sat there.

Rory spoke slowly and carefully. "Maybe before you get the Scrabble board down from the closet, you should be very clear with the other player about your house rules."

"House rules? I don't know. I tend to go with the standard rules. Nothing fancy."

Rory glugged down half her glass then took a deep breath and asked, "What about warm-up games?"

"You mean...?"

"Have you two played any other types of board games before? Did you share the crossword puzzle?"

"Do you mean the one you do with your hands? No."

Rory covered her flushing face with one hand. "So, no warm-up games."

"That depends on how you define things. The last time he came to see me at the flower shop, I did brush up against his wildcard tiles, but I didn't put my hand inside the velvet bag and grope around for anything special."

Rory hyperventilated a moment before getting herself under control. "You know what? I think you're going to be fine. Just take it slow."

Tina swirled her wine in her glass. "I'm a little worried about everything fitting together," she said.

Rory gave her a blank look. "Fitting together?"

"Most people play with seven tiles at a time because they fit on the tile rack. I think my tile rack is standard, but what if he plays with eight tiles? Or nine, or ten?"

"Tiles?" Rory didn't get it. Not yet.

Tina pressed on with the metaphor. "Rory, what if he plays with eleven tiles?" She gestured to imply a more well-endowed tile rack than the kind you'd normally expect to find with Scrabble.

Then Rory got it.

Tina knew she got it because Rory slowly leaned forward, set the wine glass on the coffee table, and then ran out of her place so fast, she left a cartoon dust cloud behind her.

"You're making great progress," Tina yelled after her best friend.

Chapter 13

Luca arrived right on time for dinner.

This time, he'd followed Tina's instructions and came around the side of the main house, right to her door.

He had flowers in his hands—a beautiful mixed flower arrangement, in a vase she recognized from her shop.

"You're kidding," she said, taking the flowers. He must have bought them on the way over, from her sister. Tina was surprised Megan hadn't sent her one of her sassy text messages, taunting her about knowing something Tina didn't know yet.

"Read the note," Luca said, glancing around the house interior before turning his beautiful blue eyes back on her.

She yanked open the envelope and pulled out one of the standard cards from the shop.

The card was in her sister's handwriting and read: SORRY I'M A JERK. - LUCA

Tina looked up, confused. Luca was grinning like crazy.

"I don't get it," she said.

"It's a precautionary measure. I'll probably do something hideous tonight."

"Like what?"

"Well, I might look around your place and ask to see the rest of it. Then you'll tell me this is all of it." He whispered, "Is this all of it?"

"Oh, I have five more rooms here. They're behind that door. Go have a look." She pointed at the coat closet. "That might seem like the standard bi-fold door of a coat closet, but it leads to the other wing of the mansion."

"I'll have to check it out later." He took the flowers and note from her hands and set them in the middle of the table. "Where is Muffins? I need to meet the famous Muffins after seeing so many pictures of him. Will he give me an autograph?"

"Muffins only stops by here when his dinner is late at the main house. He mostly lives over there, with my sister. The two of them have an intense relationship."

"Does she dress him up in outfits?"

"No," Tina said. "That might be why he likes her better."

"Just so you know, I'm not one of those guys who hates cats," Luca said. "I find them intriguing."

"Good. Because if you were one of those cat-haters, it would be a deal breaker."

"Phew. Glad I passed that test." He wrapped his arms around her and pulled her in for a kiss.

There was no one around to see them, and nowhere for Tina to escape. More importantly, she was ready to kiss him.

They kissed until she got dizzy and stumbled back, almost tipping them over.

Luca licked his lips, his gaze on her mouth. "Are you going to offer me some of that wine you're drinking?"

"I'm afraid that particular wine is all gone. It went into the sauce. Most of it, anyway. But I have another bottle I can open."

He reached into the bag he'd set down on arrival and handed her an unopened bottle. "Let's try this one."

"The bottle's dusty."

"It's from my wine cellar."

"You have a wine cellar?"

"It's where all the trendy people keep their wine."

She pointed to the closet door again. "I have a wine cellar, too. It's right through that door, in the other wing."

"Sure you do." He grabbed her and kissed her again then nuzzled his cheek against her neck. His cheek was smooth, like the cheek of someone much younger. He must have shaved right before coming over. The feeling of his skin against her neck, along with his hot breath, made her knees weak.

"You smell good," he murmured. "You smell like roast beef, which is one of my favorite smells."

She squealed and pulled away. "That's your dinner."

He pointed his finger in the air, like he'd just remembered something. "Right, dinner. I should confess. I actually ate a full dinner before I came over because I knew that your offer to make me dinner was just an excuse to get me into your lair. Your sister told me you don't use your oven to cook anything but nachos."

"I'll kill her!" Tina glared in the direction of the main house. "Did you really eat before you came over?"

He laughed. "No. I'm just teasing you. Actually, I'm famished." He plucked the note card from the table and pointed to the inscription that apologized for him being a jerk. "Now you see why I needed this. Classic jerk move, making you think I'd already had dinner."

"Try to be less of a jerk." She handed him the wine opener. "More useful, less of a jerk."

He got to work opening the bottle.

The timer for the roast went off. She pulled the enormous half-cow from the oven. Rory had brought over a new roasting pan that fit Tina's undersized oven—barely. Tina set the steaming roast on the stove top to rest before slicing. Rory had left her specific instructions for the final preparations, and Tina was doing her best to follow them.

Luca handed her a glass of wine and offered to help. He and his large frame barely fit inside the micro kitchen, let alone both of them. She shooed him out.

"Snoop around a little," she said. "I know you're dying to."

"I'm not much of a snooper," he said, but then he started looking around. He ran his hands over the wooden mantel. "This is good quality craftsmanship." Then he looked at the framed photos on the mantel above the miniature fireplace.

She realized, too late, that she should have put the photos away, or at least rearranged them.

He picked up the photo from prom. "I didn't know you were married," he said. "Please tell me you're divorced, or separated."

Her throat tightened. She was barely able to say, "That's not a bridal gown. My prom dress was pale blue, but everyone else was in much brighter colors, so I look washed out next to them."

"You look perfect," he said. "If I'd been lucky enough to be your date that night, I wouldn't have changed a thing."

"Thanks."

Tina reached for the hot roast pan without her mitts. She was lucky, and only lightly burned her fingers. She cursed under her breath and held her hand under the water faucet.

Luca was too focused on the photo to notice. "Who's the lucky guy?"

"My prom date."

"Obviously," he said. "But who is he?"

"Just a guy I used to hang out with. He was friends with my sister, too."

She pulled her hand out of the cold water, dried it off, and, like an idiot, immediately reached for the hot pan again.

This time, the burn sent a searing shock through her body. She backed up, flailing, and knocked down a metal mixing bowl. It fell to the tile floor with a clang. She swore again, louder this time, and once again turned on the cold faucet, full blast.

The pain and shock of touching the hot pan must have flipped a switch somewhere deep inside Tina. As her burned finger pulsed with pain, her usual mental defenses fell away. Everything hit her at once. Memories flooded back. Her first love pinning a blue rose corsage on her dress. His shaking hands. The photographer teasing them. The tears it seemed everyone was holding back. The blur of a wonderful evening that went by too fast.

Tina's hand throbbed from the burn. It was all too much. She collapsed forward against the sink.

She felt a hand on her back.

"Leave me alone," she said automatically.

"Did you hurt yourself?"

"Yes, but I'm fine. I just need a minute, okay? By myself."

"I can't do that," he said.

"Of course you can. I was fine for a long time before I met you, Luca."

"No, I mean there's nowhere else to go," he said. There was a long pause. "This house is too small."

Had she heard him right? Was he making a joke about her house?

Then he pulled her into his arms, into him. She crushed her face against his chest to avoid meeting his eyes. He wrapped his arms around her lower back and held her.

As quickly as Tina's emotions had flared up, they settled down again. She was breathing calmly again, breathing when Luca breathed. She was also feeling very foolish.

She pulled away and looked down at her fingertips.

"That's not too bad," she said. "Just a little red. Probably won't even blister." She pointed to the offending pan. "I grabbed that stupid thing without an oven mitt."

"Is that the only thing you're upset about?"

She wiped her eyes with a paper towel and put on a cheerful face.

"I'm fine."

"Tina, what's wrong?"

"Nothing," she said. "Except for the obvious— I'm a cheap drunk, and an emotional one."

She grabbed the glass of wine he'd poured for her, and glugged it back as proof.

"Anything else?"

"You're not the only one who doesn't behave perfectly." She pointed to her face and whisper-yelled, "SORRY I'M A JERK."

"Apology accepted," he said. "Are you sure I can't help you with anything in here? Now that I've wedged myself into your kitchen, I don't know if I can get out again."

"I guess we're stuck together. Trapped in the kitchen."

"There's nowhere I'd rather be." His gaze went to the meat. "What is that? Half a cow?"

"That's what I said when Rory... uh, popped by earlier to say hello."

He gave her a bemused look. "You mean your best friend, Rory, who works as a caterer? She just happened to pop by?"

She squeezed her way around Luca's large body and handed him the salad bowl to take to the table. "Nope. This Rory drives a garbage truck. You must be thinking of your *other* girlfriend's best friend."

"I do get all of you confused," he said.

He helped her bring the rest of the food over to the table—or at least as much as would fit on the small surface.

They sat down, and he refilled her glass.

"This is really nice of you to make me a home-cooked dinner," he said. "It's been a while since somebody took care of me like this." His eyes were shining.

She felt something in her chest, like her heart was trying to tell her something.

He cleared his throat and raised his glass, smiling and blinking rapidly.

"A toast," he said.

She raised her own glass and waited.

His voice low and soft, like a prayer, he said, "May every loving heart hear its song returned across the lake."

She was surprised by his poetic words. She was slow to clink her glass with his.

Chapter 14

After dinner and dessert, Tina said, "Let's move over to the couch."

"All the way over there? It's too far." The couch was about two feet away from the table. "I'm so full from dinner." Luca rubbed his stomach. "You'll have to carry me."

"You can stay on that swivel chair if you like, but I like to put my feet up after dinner."

Tina moved over to the couch. Luca said, "Goodbye, mushroom-shaped chair. Thank you for not breaking in half underneath me," and joined her.

It was a generous-sized couch, in an L shape. Tina could have fit a bed plus some smaller furniture inside her cottage, but she'd opted for the big sofa with a fold-out bed instead. In a small space, it was important to still have somewhere to stretch out.

When she'd bought the couch, she'd imagined having parties, and glamorous friends perching all over the stylish new sectional. In Tina's imagination, everyone wore fancy clothes and drank martinis. In reality, her friends wore socks with holes in them, and most preferred movies over parties, and popcorn over martinis. The big couch worked well for that, too, though movie nights had become less frequent now that everyone was getting married, having babies, or both.

"This is good quality upholstery," Luca said, rubbing his hands over the nubby fabric.

"We had to take the door off its hinges to get it inside. I think it's been expanding since I got it. I'm not sure I'll be able to get it out of here."

His eyes twinkled. "I'm sure you'll figure out a way. If you need someone big and strong to help, I'm your guy."

"I'll keep that in mind."

He leaned back and relaxed even more than he had been. "It's a great couch," he said. "Your kitchen is challenging, but this couch was made for me."

"It is custom made, but not for you." She batted her eyelashes. "Only because I didn't know you back then."

He let out a nervous laugh. Was he nervous? She'd been so worried about her own nerves and the averted meltdown that she hadn't given his feelings much thought. But she should have. The guy was always reminding her that big, tough guys had feelings, too.

"Would you like a coffee?" She'd picked up three kinds of beans, just for him.

"Do you see me yawning?"

"Not tonight. You must have gotten some deep sleep last night."

"I didn't," he said. "Being here with you is better than caffeine."

He reached over and lightly touched her arm, then her shoulder, then her hair. He gently pushed his fingers into her curly hair, but he wisely didn't try to comb through and get himself caught in the knots. He lightly massaged his fingertips on the back of her head then pulled his hand away.

Tina stared at his cheek. His shave lookcd really close to the skin. He looked brand new, like a clone in a sci-fi movie who'd just come out of an egg. And he smelled like heaven.

"Thanks again for the flowers," she told him.

"I didn't just bring you flowers."

"Oh, right. Thanks for the wine, too. It was excellent. You must have a well-stocked wine cellar."

"I also brought you this." He leaned back to pull something from his jeans pocket. A jewelry box. It was bigger than a ring box, but smaller than a necklace box.

Tina's hands trembled as she reached for the velvet case. Jewelry? On the fourth date? None of the dating advice websites had prepared her for a jewelry scenario.

"Open it. Open it now," he said, sounding like an excited kid on Christmas day.

She snapped open the box. Inside was a charm bracelet, with several charms already connected to it. She pulled the bracelet out. One charm was a tiny little hammer. There was also a kangaroo, a motorbike, a flower pot, and a tea cup. The charms were all symbols of things connected to them and that they'd talked about.

She waved one hand to fan her face. "Luca, this is too much. I don't know what to say."

"Tell me it's cute." He tapped the tea cup with the end of his fingernail. "This one is the most cute, and you know I'm not a man who uses the word *cute* lightly."

"It is cute," she said. "It's exactly like the tea cups they have at Delilah's." Tina's view of the bracelet and its tiny charms grew blurry. She blinked furiously. "You really brought your A game to the fourth date," she said. "I feel so bad. I didn't even make you dinner myself. Rory did all the prep work."

"Then I can't take full credit for this," he said. "I just bought the thing. I didn't make the charms."

"Technically, I didn't pay for dinner. Rory insisted."

"But you hosted," he said. "I'm giving you full credit for a great dinner, whether you agree with it or not."

He took the bracelet from her hand and undid the clasp. She held out her hand, which no longer hurt from the burn, and he fastened the bracelet around her wrist.

She admired the bracelet, turning her wrist back and forth. "I wish I'd gotten you something," she said.

"Tina, you made me dinner, plus you've already given me so much. This dark cloud of dread has been hanging over me since I got the keys to the garage."

"What dark cloud of dread?"

"The idea of me, running a business. It's crazy. When I picked up the keys from the real estate agent, I was sure I'd made the worst decision of my life. Everything felt wrong. But then I met you, and things turned around. You turned it around. Now I feel like I'm finally on the right path."

She waved her charm bracelet. "Sounds like I'm your good-luck charm."

He laughed at her dumb joke then kissed her. The kissing went from warm to hot quickly. He pulled away and gave her a serious look.

"You want to hear something funny? I started thinking about charms the day I met you, but I told myself to be cool and not scare you away. I wanted to get you those charms, but I promised myself I'd wait until our fourth date, assuming I even got that far."

"Is that why you kept talking about which date we were on?"

"That's it." He frowned. "Why? What did you think?"

"I thought that by the fourth date, it might be time for us to play Scrabble."

He smiled and stretched his arms out along the back of the sofa. "I'll play whatever you like."

Chapter 15

Tina Gardenia prepared for a typical Sunday afternoon routine.

Rory arrived a few minutes early and sent a text message saying she was at the main house. The girls were planning to do laundry together, as they had done about one Sunday per month for many years.

When the message came in, Tina was still sorting her laundry—mostly just trying to find it. The tiny home didn't have conventional closets, so she had to stuff things in nooks and crannies and other creative spaces. While tidying for her dinner with Luca the day before, she'd gotten so creative that she couldn't locate any of her socks. She invited Rory to come around to the small house and meet her there.

Rory pushed open the door to the tiny home and entered cautiously. She'd left her laundry at the main house and was carrying the usual: a big takeout cup full of coffee and a box of gourmet donuts. She visually scoured the house interior like a detective searching for clues. She sniffed then wrinkled her nose as she walked over to the door for the bathroom, which she flung open.

Rory demanded, "Where is he? Is he hiding?"

"Luca's not here," Tina said. "And where would he hide, anyway? This place is basically one room."

"One room plus a closet." Rory flung open the home's only closet. It was full, but only with stuff.

Tina spotted her dirty socks on the hat shelf and grabbed them.

"I told you," Tina said. "He's not here. You're going to meet him, but I swear it won't be by ambush."

"He must be nearby. I can smell him."

Rory closed the closet door then yanked it open a second time.

"He's not in there," Tina said. "And he's not in the main house, either. I promised I wouldn't spring him on you before you're ready, and I won't."

"Okay. I believe you." She pushed back her curly hair and tied it up with an elastic. Hair nets were for cooking, but elastics were for laundry day.

Tina finished retrieving dirty laundry from the various places she'd hidden it before dinner the night before.

"So?" Rory held out both hands. "Let's get it over with. How was last night?"

"Wow. I'm so excited to tell my best friend about my recent date, especially when she's clearly so enthused."

"This is me, being supportive," Rory said. "How was the roast beef?"

"Perfect. I used the drippings to make the gravy, like you told me to."

"How was the salad?"

"It was salad."

"How was the cheesecake?"

"Very sweet, but perfect, as always. You are the best caterer in the entire city."

"And?"

Tina played coy for a moment before saying, "We did play Scrabble last night."

Rory's body tensed, but she didn't run. "And?"

"His board strategy is more aggressive than I'm used to, but I liked it."

Rory looked down at her shoes, her cheeks turning red. "I'm happy for you," she mumbled.

"I'm being honest with you," Tina said. "We played Scrabble."

Rory frowned and turned redder. "I heard you the first time."

Tina picked up the slim cardboard box that had been under a pile of dirty laundry on the coffee table. It was the Scrabble board she usually kept in the closet.

"We played this." Tina shook the box, making the tiles rattle.

"Oh," Rory said. "Oh. Oh!"

"Yeah," Tina said. "The fourth date is when you play Scrabble. That's a new house rule."

Rory swayed back and forth, still on the verge of being overwhelmed.

Tina tossed her dirty laundry into the basket she'd brought over from the main house. "This should be everything," she said. "It has to be, since these are all the clothes I own." She headed for the door. "Let's do some laundry!"

Rory took one more look at the Scrabble box, then at the coat closet, then followed Tina out.

The girls walked over to the main house, where they found Tina's sister, Megan Gardenia, in the kitchen, doing some baking. The flower shop was closed Sundays, except for major events like Mother's Day, so the sisters usually had Sundays off together. They sometimes hung out, if they were getting along that weekend.

Megan was making bread. She said to Tina, "Mom phoned from Italy, and you'll never guess."

"Please don't make me guess," Tina said. "Just tell me for once."

"The gossip about you and Luca has gone global." Megan waggled her eyebrows. "Mom knows."

"Oh, crap."

"It gets better." Megan grinned as she punched down bread dough. "You know that game where people whisper things, and the story changes with each person it goes through? Anyway, Mom thinks you're dating the leader of a crime family."

Rory leaned on the counter, listening without comment.

Tina said, "The leader of a crime family? How did she get that?"

"Someone on the telephone chain made the leap from motorbike repair to biker gang, and it must have exploded from there. You should have heard how worked up she was. She was threatening to come home."

"I hope you talked her down," Tina said. "I refuse to be held responsible for cutting short her fabulous year abroad."

Megan snorted. "She's not cutting anything short. If anything, she might not come back. She's sharing her apartment with someone. A guy. She told me that when they share the bed, it's platonic, because they sleep foot to head."

At the mention of sleeping foot to head—another of Rory's hot button issues, though one that rarely came up in conversation—Rory let out a strangled cry then bolted away to the laundry room.

Megan stared after Tina's friend. "Is *that* still happening?"

"Be nice," Tina said. "She's making progress. Yesterday, she said *pantyhose*."

"Speaking of pantyhose, how was your date last night? I noticed you pulled the blinds shut after dinner."

"Spying again? You need to get a life."

"Couldn't help myself. That roast looked good. I was going to come over and mooch around for some leftovers, but I noticed the whole cottage was rocking on its foundations. Was there a small earthquake last night? One that was extremely localized underneath you?"

"The cottage was not rocking." It had been built out of a former garage. Unlike tiny homes that were built on wheels, the cottage hadn't rocked because it couldn't have.

"From over here, it sure looked like it was bouncing like a trampoline. Must have been the wind."

"Or someone's imagination."

"I may have implied to Mom that she should have an inspector check the foundation when she gets back. You know, in case you and your boyfriend from the crime syndicate cracked the seismic upgrades."

"Meenie! We were playing Scrabble."

"Sure you were," Megan said. "Does he have a brother?"

"I don't know. He doesn't talk much about his family. Whenever I ask, he turns it around and asks about mine."

"You can't blame the guy," Megan said. "Your sister is pretty interesting."

Tina pulled out her phone and checked for messages. The night before, when Luca had lodged his large body in the kitchen and insisted on helping with the dishes, he had mentioned getting up early to meet a new subcontractor at the garage.

As for messages, there was nothing from Luca.

Tina had an excuse to contact him first, so she typed: *My sister Megan asked me if you happen to have a brother. I'm only asking because if you do, we need to warn him about her.*

"And send," Tina said as she touched the button to send the text.

"You sound exactly like Mom when you talk to your phone like that. Or Grandma. I swear you're twenty-nine going on seventy."

Tina heard the sound of Rory starting the washing machine down the hallway. Tina continued staring at her phone, waiting to hear from Luca.

Megan noticed and said, "Give him a minute to get back to you, stalker. I'm sure he'll still have a brother if you put your phone away."

"You're the stalker," Tina said. "Don't spy on me, and don't start rumors with Mom."

"I didn't start the rumors. You two are the talk of the neighborhood. If you want to keep your little romance with the crime boss a secret, try riding that big bike of his over to the other side of town."

Tina shook her finger angrily. "If Mom calls again, you'd better set her straight."

Megan sighed. "I already did."

Tina dropped her finger. "Thanks." Megan wasn't *actually* the worst, so Tina had figured as much.

Megan went back to her baking, and Tina wandered off to do her laundry with Rory.

Tina and Rory's Sunday-afternoon laundry routine hadn't changed much over the past decade. In between folding loads from the dryer, they lazed around in the TV room, watching movies and eating donuts. It couldn't have been that bad for them. They were *gourmet* donuts with fancy flavor combinations. The kind of donuts that social media influencers posted photos of online.

Later, after Rory left, Tina checked her phone for the thousandth time.

There was still no response from Luca.

Had she touched on a nerve, mentioning a brother? Was he just really busy? Was he ignoring her? Had he dropped his phone in a toilet? Had he been abducted by aliens?

Tina carried her folded laundry back out to the cottage and put everything away in the various storage spots.

The charms jingled around her wrist.

She checked her phone again. No response.

The flowers from the night before were sitting on the table, next to the note he'd used to pre-apologize for being a jerk.

Tina played with the charms on her wrist. The symbols were all cute, except for the kangaroo, which looked a little menacing.

The bracelet was such a thoughtful, personal gift. Luca had really made her feel special.

She thought back to the first time she'd met Luca, when she'd warned him that no woman on earth wanted to get "the usual."

He certainly hadn't given her "the usual" last night. In addition to the Scrabble game, there had been other fun activities for grown-ups. Nothing that would have, as Megan put it, cracked the cottage's seismic upgrades. Nothing that Tina regretted. At least not until now, the next day, when Luca hadn't even sent a single message.

Was this his big flaw? Was Luca Lowell the kind of guy who lost interest after the chase was over? Was this why he had to buy so many apology bouquets?

Chapter 16

Monday morning, Tina dug through the stack of jeans she kept in the drawer under her oven to pick out the day's outfit. Luca still hadn't returned her text message from the day before, and every minute that passed was bringing her down. She grabbed her pair of ratty cut-offs and her stained sweatshirt and slammed the drawer shut.

She left the charm bracelet on the bathroom counter and strapped on a gold watch—an old gift from the father who wasn't in her life.

She stepped outside, immediately changed her mind, and ran back inside. She tossed the gold watch on the couch on the way to the bathroom then put on the charm bracelet. For luck. Then she swapped out the extra-large sweatshirt for another one that was still too large, but not as stained.

All her indecision was making her late for work, plus the late-spring sky was gray and threatening rain, so she drove her car to work instead of walking.

She drove past Ralph's Garage slowly, looking for any sign of Luca. The windows were still covered in paper, so she couldn't see anything.

The sign for the garage had been upgraded and looked perfect for the neighborhood. Luca hired a guy who specialized in hand-painting signs to come in and spruce up the letters. The sign artist also added a line about motorbikes, exactly as Tina had suggested.

Tina opened the flower store—only fifteen minutes late—and tried to keep herself busy and her mind off Luca. Her heart still skipped a beat every time someone came in the door.

It was lunch time when a blond woman Tina didn't recognize came in.

The woman pretended to be looking at the new ferns and orchids, but her browsing behavior wasn't normal. She looked at each plant with the same amount of time, and she kept sneaking looks at the florist.

Tina said, "Are you looking for an orchid today?"

"Just looking," the blond woman said, then she quickly scuttled back out again.

Tina pulled out her phone and checked it again. No messages from Luca.

Even though he hadn't replied to her previous joke text about her sister, Tina sent him a new text message:*Have you been sending spies over here to the flower shop?*

To her surprise, he responded immediately: *No. Why?*

She frowned at the phone. She should have been glad he replied, but this wasn't the sort of sweet, romantic message she'd been hoping for.

Tina: *Some blonde chick was just in here staring at me.*

She waited five minutes for a response and didn't get one.

The door chimed again. She looked up, expecting to see Luca, coming to surprise her with something thoughtful.

Instead, she got the blond woman back.

This time, rather than pretending to look at the plants, the blonde walked right up to Tina at the counter and shoved the screen of her phone at Tina's face.

The blonde asked, "Did you make this?"

There was a photo of flowers on the screen. Tina recognized the raffia tie from Gardenia Flowers' regular supply. More importantly, she recognized the extravagant arrangement. It was the one Luca had dropped a bundle on the first time he'd visited the shop.

Tina took a better look at the blonde, meeting her ice-blue eyes. The woman was older than Tina, maybe forty, but really pretty, like a Barbie doll. She'd had her eyebrows done with the trendy new style.

Tina answered cautiously. "Ma'am, if the arrangement came with one of our cards, then it must have been prepared by either me or my coworker."

"I saw Luca Lowell in here two weeks ago," the woman said.

Tina didn't give anything away.

"He was talking to the other girl who works here," the blonde said. "It was busy in here, and he was behind the counter. It looked like he was helping her sell flowers."

Tina stayed quiet. On the Wednesday before last, Luca had been there, helping Megan sell out the store so that Tina had no choice Thursday morning but to go for breakfast with Luca. That had been their first date. Number one.

The blonde tapped—or scratched—the counter with her long nails. She wore thick gel nails. She had an angry tigress energy. Tina quickly assessed that this woman was one of Luca's exes, one of the women he was a jerk to. This was the woman who'd been angry at Luca, and now it seemed she was angry at Tina, too.

"Luca was in here selling flowers," the angry blonde said. "Wasn't he?"

Tina feigned ignorance. "Who? Someone named Lucas?"

Angry Blonde squinted at Tina's face. "The other girl's your sister, isn't she?"

"Yes," Tina said. "My sister works here with me. She'll actually be here any minute now. I'm sure she'd be happy to help you." Tina looked at the door. *Any minute now*, she thought. *Please show up early today, Megan. Please walk in the door right now.*

Angry Blonde said, "And you both know Luca Lowell. He bought Ralph's Garage. Everyone on this street knows about him."

Tina snapped her fingers. "Oh! You mean Luca. The guy who bought the garage. He's been getting to know some of the people who work up and down the street. For business networking, I guess."

The woman leaned on the counter. "You'd better warn your sister," she hissed.

Tina took a step back, out of face-stabbing range. The counter was between them, but those gel nails added half an inch of reach.

Tina lifted her chin and asked, "Warn my sister about what?" Tina was cautious, but she didn't scare that easily. Her wrestling opponents in high school had learned that.

The woman's face contorted with rage. In a low, threatening tone, she said, "You tell your sister that Luca Lowell is nothing but trouble. He's a tease and a liar."

"Good to know," Tina said. She was too focused on the woman for it to register instantly, but it did start to sink in. A tease and a liar? That wasn't the Luca she knew.

The woman was suddenly grabbing Tina by the wrist. "What's this?" Angry Blonde demanded. "Is this a motorbike charm? Is this from *him*? From Luca?"

Tina yanked her wrist free. "Excuse me?" Tina could fight, but she also had manners, unlike the other woman.

The woman glared at her. "Luca gave that to you," she said. "Didn't he?"

Tina hid the charm bracelet behind her back. "My jewelry is none of your business," she said. "If you're not here to buy flowers, please leave. I have a lot of work to do."

Angry Blonde retreated slowly, or at least she appeared to be retreating. She didn't get far before she side-stepped around a greeting card display and entered the staff-only area. She was behind the counter now.

The instant the woman crossed the yellow line that marked off the staff-only area of the store, it was like a bell going off in Tina's head.

What Angry Blonde didn't know was that back in high school, when Tina and Megan's friends were learning cheers and running around in pleated skirts, Megan and Tina were learning how to pin down opponents.

Angry Blonde went down like a house of cards. Tina held her down to buy a few seconds to think. Angry Blonde, who was now Confused Blonde, groaned and tried to fight her way out of the hold, but she didn't have a chance.

The door chimed.

Was it Megan, early for her shift?

No.

It was Luca Lowell. "Hello?" He looked around the shop, which must have appeared to be empty. "Is anyone here? The door was open."

"I'm down here," Tina said. She was using her body weight to keep Confused Blonde from doing any damage with her tigress nails, but the top of her head would have been visible if Luca knew where to look. "Behind the counter."

"What are you doing down there?" He walked around at a leisurely pace then froze in his motorcycle boots as he surveyed the scene. "Who's that? Is that who I think it is?" He pointed at the blonde who was immobilized underneath Tina.

"I don't know," Tina said.

"You don't know?"

"This isn't what it looks like!"

"It's not?" He stepped over the blonde's flailing legs, hooked his hands under Tina's armpits, and gently lifted her off the blonde. "Because it looks to me like you've got my former real estate agent in a headlock."

"It wasn't a headlock," Tina said. "It was a chicken wing pin."

"A what? Have you lost your mind?"

"Luca, she came at me! I had no choice."

The blonde, who'd gotten to her feet, glared at both of them. "I'm pressing charges," she said.

Luca stepped between the women, facing the blonde, and said, "No. You're not." He crossed his arms.

Then the woman cursed him. Not with swear words. She literally cursed him. "Curse you, Luca Lowell!"

Gruffly, he said, "Leave now, and we won't press charges against you."

She cursed him again, this time with swear words.

Then she leaned to the side and spat at Tina, which nearly got her an ankle pick takedown, but luckily for her and the seven gel fingernails that hadn't been snapped yet, Luca held Tina back.

The woman kicked over a ficus tree and stormed out of the flower store.

Chapter 17

Luca's eyes were burning bright as he stared at Tina Gardenia, the wrestler.

"Remind me not to get on your bad side," he said.

"Too late," Tina said. "You are on my bad side. But don't worry. I'm not going to go crazy and stalk your new girlfriends."

"My new girlfriends?" He thumbed at the door. "You don't think Jessica is one of my exes, do you?"

"I thought she was a little old for you, but yeah. What did you do to her?" Tina held up her hand. "Wait. Don't tell me. I don't want to know."

"Tina, I did not and would not date a woman like Jessica. That woman has red flags all over her. She tried, trust me. She showed up at my place with a bottle of wine, but I made it very clear I wasn't interested."

Tina crossed her arms. "I'm not an idiot, Luca."

"No, you're not. And you're not weak, either. Obviously."

"Your story doesn't check out. If you never dated her and you rejected all her advances, why did you buy her that nice apology bouquet?"

"It's kind of a long story. It's hard to explain."

Tina glanced over at the door. "I don't see anyone else I need to pin down and immobilize at the moment, so why don't you try?"

"That woman—Jessica Fitzgibbon—is a real estate agent. As you may know, real estate is a tough business. It's not like your business, where you do a high volume of low-value sales. For a real estate broker, every deal has the potential to make or break their month, maybe their year."

"I know how sales commissions work, Luca," Tina said impatiently.

"Jessica's family owns a new coffee chain that's opening up locations all over the city. They're expanding aggressively. The Fitzgibbons are *very* aggressive."

"That, I can believe." She waved her hand for him to keep going.

"Jessica was the listing agent for Ralph's Garage. She put it up for sale, but she wasn't actively looking for an arms-length buyer. She was waiting for the owners to get frustrated and agree to a lowball deal with the Fitzgibbon family. They would have knocked the building to the ground before the ink on the demolition permit was dry. Then you'd have a generic chain coffee store on the corner, and Ralph and his family wouldn't have the equity they deserved."

"And you stopped that from happening? How?"

"I went around Jessica and negotiated directly with Ralph. It was perfectly legal. Jessica put up a fuss when she heard about our deal. We went out for drinks, once, and she tried to negotiate her way into the day, and a commission. I said it was up to Ralph, but then he was so furious when he found out what she was up to, he threatened to sue her. There was no way he was going to give her a single penny. I might have thrown a little cash her way, just to cover the costs of the lousy advertising she'd done, but then she came over with a bottle of wine, tottering around my place in her spiky heels, and I decided I didn't want anything to do with her."

"You mean after you kicked her out of bed the next morning, right?"

He looked hurt. "Tina, who do you think I am?"

"You tell me. That woman wasn't just mad about a lost business deal. It was personal."

"I may have led her on a little," he said sheepishly. "She did throw herself at me. I got confused. But I didn't sleep with her."

"You didn't?"

"With Jessica? I got confused, but I'm not an idiot. What kind of guy do you think I am?"

"I think you're the kind of guy who plays Scrabble with a girl and doesn't text her the next day."

"Oh." He looked down at his boots. "I did get your message on Sunday."

"Well? Why didn't you text me back?"

"I'm not good at that," he said. "Texting. It's not my thing."

"You were pretty good at texting when you were setting up dates with me."

"Yeah." He looked away. "I had some help from the woman who was setting up my accounting system. She doesn't work on Sundays."

"You blew me off all day because your accountant wasn't available to help you compose the perfect text message?"

He winced. "She's actually more of a bookkeeper."

Tina didn't know what to say, so she said nothing.

"I came by the flower shop, but it was Sunday, and you weren't here."

"That's why the hours on the door for Sunday just say *maybe*." She shook her head. "You walked up the street to come here, but you couldn't take a minute to send me a single text message?"

He looked her in the eyes. "Come on, Tina. It wouldn't have just been one message. I might have pulled it together for the first couple, but eventually I would have said something wrong, and then it would be there, on the record, where I couldn't take it back."

Tina shook her head. "You really don't know the first thing about women, do you?"

"My mother passed away when I was five. I was raised by my father and uncle. I only know two things about women, and that's all I need to know."

She had to know. "What two things?"

"That I *like* women, and that the best kind is one that's cute. Like you." He batted his eyelashes. "Just you."

"For a big, tough guy, you sure say the word *cute* a lot."

"You win," he said.

"What do I win?"

"My heart."

He reached into his pocket and handed her a tiny, heart-shaped charm.

"It's pretty small for such a big guy," she said. "Did you buy that today? I didn't think the jewelry store was open on Mondays."

"I had it before," he explained. "I didn't want to scare you, so I took it off the bracelet before I gave it to you." He looked at the tiny heart in her palm. "Isn't it cute?"

It was cute. So cute, and such a sweet gesture, that Tina stopped worrying about exactly how confused he'd been the night Jessica Fitzgibbon visited his place. Jessica Fitzgibbon didn't have Luca's heart. Tina did.

"Now you have my heart," he said. "Promise you won't break it."

Tina attempted to hold onto the heart while unclasping the charm bracelet, but her arms were rubbery from pinning Jessica Fitzgibbon by her chicken wings. Tina fumbled the heart and dropped it on the floor.

Luca frowned at her. "That's not a good sign." He crouched down and grabbed the heart charm then, instead of handing it back to her, tucked it into his pocket.

Tina said, "Really?"

"You dropped it," he said. "That's a sign. You're not ready yet."

"Give me the charm."

"No." He stepped back slowly, grinning, and started making his way out of the shop. "Are you going to be okay here without any adult supervision?"

"My sister will be here any minute now. Not that I need supervision! And what do you mean, *adult*? You're only a couple years older than me, mister."

"In a few years, you'll know what I mean." He winked. "I should get back to the garage. Let me know if any of my other stalkers come by."

"You know I will."

And then he left.

Tina checked the calendar to see if it was a full moon. She was not surprised to find that it was. She'd had some weird Monday mornings, but that one took the cake.

Chapter 18

Megan Gardenia strolled in late to take over at the flower store.

"You're early," Tina said with a snort. "For Tuesday's shift."

Megan gave her sister a flat look. "There's a rip in your sweatshirt."

"I had to wrestle a customer."

"Did you win?"

Tina grinned. "You wanna see the broken gel fingernail tips she left in the floor mat?"

"You know I do."

Megan examined the victory trophies while Tina told her about the morning's excitement.

Megan's takeaway was "So, he doesn't have a brother. That's too bad."

"Focus, Meenie. Luca bought two arrangements, and they were for different women. Who do you think the second one was for?"

Megan frowned. "The second flowers were for his more hardcore stalker. The one who's going to murder you. You'd better sleep with one eye open."

"Thanks. You've been super helpful, as always."

Megan took a bow.

Tina gathered her things, passed along the instructions about the day's orders and deliveries, and left the shop.

Outside on the sidewalk, the sun was shining again. Tina's charm bracelet glinted in the light.

She thought about the cute little heart, and how she wanted to earn it back.

She walked up Baker Street to Ralph's Garage.

Tina's heart began beating rapidly, even though she was walking at a slow pace. What an adventure the day was turning into. It was no wonder her nervous system was so excitable. It wasn't every day she wrestled a real estate agent.

She took a detour into Bookworm Books to catch her breath. Tina's curvy blonde cousin, Peaches Monroe, was leaning on the counter, reading a paperback novel. Peaches was twenty-one, lived with her best friend who was the same age, and always had plenty of interesting stories.

Tina asked, "What are you reading?"

Peaches closed the book quickly. "Just trash," she said. "I have terrible taste in books." She wrinkled her nose and grinned. "And boys."

"You're still so young," Tina said. "I'm sure your taste will mature, from boys to men."

Peaches raised her eyebrows. "Speaking of men, have you seen the big hunk of man who took over Ralph's Garage? He looks like he lifts the bikes over his head on his lunch breaks for exercise. Nice eyes, too."

Butterflies fluttered in Tina's stomach. So much for temporarily taking her mind off Luca Lowell.

"I may know who you're talking about," Tina said coolly.

Peaches saw right through her older cousin's bluff. "You!" She pointed her finger at Tina. "I knew the rumors were true. You two are an item!"

"Not exactly."

"Well, you'd better grab him before someone else does. Or before Megan scares him away from the entire family."

"I'll take that under advisement," Tina said.

Some customers entered the bookstore, so Tina said goodbye and turned to leave.

Peaches yelled out, "You go get him, girl. And make me a bridesmaid. I've always wanted to be a bridesmaid. I promise I won't even complain about the dress!"

Tina waved for her cousin to calm down, then left the bookstore. She was hit with a strong aroma of vanilla and sugar. Donut Joe's was right next door.

Tina popped in, got a donut, and chatted casually with Rhonda until Rhonda, like Peaches, also started talking about the attractive new owner of Ralph's Garage.

Rhonda cackled and said, in her gravelly voice, "I wouldn't kick a man like that out of bed for eating crackers, if you know what I mean. I wouldn't even care if he looked at other, younger women, as long as he looked at me sometimes. Those eyes of his..."

Tina asked, "Are you dating anyone, Rhonda?"

"Don't you worry about me," Rhonda said with a hand wave. "I've got my cat, and that's all I need to be happy."

"Cats are great," Tina said. She thanked Rhonda for the chat and continued on her way.

After a few stops into other stores, and a few chats with other local business owners and workers, Tina finally reached Ralph's Garage.

There was still paper all over the windows, so she couldn't see in. She tried the door. It was unlocked. She went in.

Inside, the old reception area had been changed so much, it was unrecognizable. A couple of guys were working on assembling a counter, and a few more were painting.

Luca looked up from some blueprints, broke out in a grin, then frowned and tried to shoo her out. "Nothing's finished," he said. "I don't want you to see it before it's ready."

"Luca, I have enough visual imagination to see things that aren't completely done yet," she said.

"Fine," he said with a sigh. "Sorry about the mess. Nothing's finished, but it is coming together."

Tina took a few more steps in and looked around the rejuvenated space in awe. The old drop ceiling with water-stained acoustic tiles had been removed, and the exposed wood beams had been sandblasted clean. Everything new was a different shade of gray, with chrome accents and a few splashes of color. A painter was putting a glossy coat of red on the wooden window frames.

"Red window frames," Tina said. "Just like my house."

"They were going to be gray, like the columns, but then a visit to a certain florist's private residence made me change my mind."

"Luca, this isn't a garage anymore."

He nodded toward the service bays, which were newly visible from the reception, now that an entire wall had been removed and replaced with glass.

"Not yet, I know," Luca said. "We're still waiting on some equipment."

"Forget the equipment. I'm getting my couch and moving in here. This isn't a garage. It's my dream home."

"But you already have a garage that you live in. It suits you. It's cute."

She looked around the giant space again, awestruck. "I'm not sure *cute* is going to suit me much longer. I may be outgrowing a few things."

They were interrupted by the men working on the counter needing to ask Luca about something.

"Stick around awhile," Luca said to her. "I'll have someone run out and get your favorite tea. We've got a kettle and everything." He waved at a folding table with a pile of takeout food containers, disposable cups, and one grimy plug-in kettle.

"Another time," Tina said. "I'll let you focus on your work."

"Before you go, save me from bugging my bookkeeper to help me text you. How's Friday night? Would Muffins mind if you came to my house for dinner? Fair's fair, and you made me dinner already."

"Sure. And then, on Saturday, I won't phone you or text you. Fair's fair."

The men who'd been working on the counter were still standing there, looking at the ceiling and pretending not to be listening.

Luca grinned. "Maybe on Saturday, that won't be a problem because you'll still be at my house."

Tina shook her head and left.

Chapter 19

Tina Gardenia drove across town and pulled her car onto Luca's street at quarter to seven.

She had permanently retired her ugly oversized sweatshirts and was wearing a relatively new stretchy top with jeans. The charm bracelet Luca gave her was sparkling on her left wrist with its cute charms.

Summer had arrived. Bright sunshine still glinted off car trim, mirrors, and windows along the street.

This was a family-oriented neighborhood. Half the front lawns were strewn with giant plastic toys. The scent of barbecue hung in the air.

Luca's house was neither the newest nor the oldest on the block. It had been built in an architectural style that was popular in the city during the seventies, with minimal decoration—just a box with a low-pitched roof.

Next door to Luca's, a man in a hat was watering some shrubs in the front yard. He watched Tina as she parked her car and then walked up to Luca's front door.

The man called out, "You must be Tina." He dropped the garden hose and reached across the shrubs to shake her hand. "I'm Chris. I'm the local heirloom tomato supplier. If you need salsa, just let me know."

Luca opened his door. "Chris! Let her get in the door before you start pushing your condiments, man."

Chris laughed then looked Tina evenly in the eyes. "Do you like chutney?"

She replied, "Is that the stuff with raisins?" She wrinkled her nose.

"Never mind," Chris said. "My chutney is not for you. But you do like salsa, right? Everyone loves salsa."

"I probably eat salsa twice a week," Tina said.

Luca walked over and draped his arm across her shoulders. It was a casual gesture, but the touch of his arm, combined with the sunshine and the friendly neighbor, was almost too perfect.

Luca kissed Tina on the side of her forehead, and then the three of them chatted for a while about the plans Chris had for a new greenhouse.

A woman popped her head out of the neighbor's house and said, "Chris, let those two have their dinner already! Would you stop bothering them about the tomatoes? Some people have other interests."

Chris said to Tina, "I'll save some of my next batch of salsa for you. You can get it from Luca, if he doesn't eat it all first."

Tina thanked him, then Chris picked up the garden hose again and wished them a good dinner.

Luca led Tina into his house then shut the door behind them.

Tina hadn't even gotten a peek around inside before he started kissing her, backing her up against the door.

She giggled and ducked under his arm to escape. Her first peek was at what should have been a living room, but looked like a motorbike showroom.

"Luca, why do you have motorbikes parked in your house where a living room should be?"

He replied, "I'd put them in the guest bedroom, but it's tricky getting them up and down the stairs."

"But shouldn't they be in a garage? Or outside?"

"This is *my* house," he said. "At your house, you keep pants in your oven drawer. At my house, I have bikes in the front room."

"Do you ride the bikes around inside the house?" She walked over to one that looked like the bike from the movie set and touched the shiny chrome.

"Gotta ride somewhere when the weather's bad outside." He joined her by the bike and used a black cloth to wipe the spot she'd just touched. "Of course I don't ride them inside the house. I wouldn't want the engine exhaust getting upstairs."

"Right. Because that would be crazy."

"My house, my rules."

She moved toward a hallway. He caught her by the hand and held her back. "Where are you going? There's nothing but bikes down here on the lower level."

"You're kidding."

"Do you want to give me a hard time about how I choose to live, or do you want to come upstairs and see the regular living space?"

She shrugged. "I can give you a hard time about the upstairs."

Still holding her hand, he led her up a central staircase.

The upper floor looked more like a regular house. Mainly because there were no motorbikes.

"This house was originally a duplex," he explained as he walked her over to the kitchen. "I did a full reno on the kitchen two years ago." He slapped the poured concrete counter.

The finishes were all steel, concrete, and sturdy-looking wood. "And what a renovation it was. It's so masculine. One might call it a man-ovation."

He raised an eyebrow. "I didn't know we were already at the pun stage of the relationship. I suppose next you'll be shaving your legs with my razor."

"We are on the fifth date," she said. "The fifth date is for bad puns. Stealing your razor doesn't happen for a while."

"I'm glad someone knows the routine."

She took a good look around the house. It was very open, with few interior divisions. The walls were bare of pictures, and all the furniture was black and leather. It screamed *single man*, which was appropriate.

"Luca, your house is really nice. I've never dated anyone who lived in a house they owned. You're an actual grown-up."

"Tell me about the guys you usually date." He lifted the lid off a pot on the stove and stirred something. "While you tell me about them, look away while I hide the store-bought jar this sauce just came out of."

She took a seat on a tall chrome chair and looked away as asked.

"My previous boyfriends were definitely a type. Nice guys. I know you don't want to hear about them. You're just being polite."

Luca kept stirring at the stove. "If they were so nice, what happened? Do you not like nice guys?"

"You got me. All this time I've been single, I was secretly pining for Bad Boy Biker Boys. I'm holding out for one with a very special tattoo."

"Oh?"

"The tattoo's got to have three things. Bullets, barbed wire, and battleships."

He let out a long whistle. "I'd hate to run into that guy in a dark alley."

"I'm sure you'd be able to hold your own."

"I might, if you teach me some of your wrestling moves." He picked up a red apron from the concrete counter and pulled it on over his head. "Tell me about your friends," he said. "Are they into guys with tattoos of bullets, barbed wire, and battleships?"

"No, just regular guys. And except for Rory, all my friends are getting married and having babies."

"Is that something you want?"

"Ew," she said.

He brought her a glass of wine.

"Ew?"

"I dunno," she said. "Eventually. Like, way, way off in the future. We don't have to talk about this stuff now. We're only on date number five."

"The date for bad puns," he said.

"Exactly."

She took a sip of the wine. Suddenly, the house felt very warm.

None of the dating advice websites had prepared Tina for the fifth date. The next milestone was a year from now, when it was time to trick the guy into thinking he wanted to marry her. The articles were so stupid. And yet she always read them.

Luca announced that the sauce was hot and it was time to move to the table.

"Where?" She glanced around. The kitchen led to two other spaces. "I'm so used to my ridiculously small place, where everything is within arm's distance."

He reached out and hugged her to his side. "That's it," he said. "That's what I love about your place. There's nowhere for you to get away."

She kissed him then pulled away. She took a guess at where the dining room was, and was right.

He served dinner, and they ate while making light conversation about business comings and goings on Baker Street.

Tina didn't feel as comfortable as she did around her family or friends. She wasn't as nervous as she'd been on the fourth date, but she was nervous enough to have a light burning sensation at the front of her throat. Was it Luca? He was being perfectly charming, paying attention to her, but not too much. If it wasn't him, then it had to be the house. It was so big. So adult.

Maybe there was a reason she usually dated man-children who spent their social lives online. Those guys didn't intimidate her. They didn't make her feel like she wasn't doing enough with her life. She wasn't exactly a go-getter. She was twenty-nine and lived with her mother, working the same job she'd had for a decade.

Tina had looked up the term *arrested development*, which was more than just the name of a TV show, and had discovered that she might be the poster girl.

The conversation shifted to Luca's renovations at Ralph's Garage.

"We're already taking bookings for the first month," Luca said, suddenly picking up her plate.

She stared at the plate in surprise. It was empty. Was she already done with eating? She'd been so busy holding up her end of the small talk while beating herself up in her head that she wasn't sure she'd tasted the pasta. She hadn't exactly been fully present.

Why couldn't she be more present and in the moment all the time, like Luca?

He finished loading the dishwasher then returned and held out his hand.

"Come on," he said, helping her up. "Let's go downstairs, and you can have your pick for our after-dinner ride."

"Our what?"

"There's nothing like an after-dinner ride," he said. "This is why I didn't have any wine. I'm good to drive. All you need to do is pick out which bike you want to take for a spin."

He led her back down the stairs, to all the motorbikes. It was still a shock to see bikes inside a house, but less of a shock than the first time.

She took him over to the bike they'd rode on their second date, to the movie set. "This one's my favorite," she said without hesitation.

His face lit up, as though she'd just passed a test. With flying colors.

He leaned over the bike, his muscles rippling, and started rolling it. "There's a ramp at the back door," he said.

She ran ahead of him, located the back door, and opened it for him.

Luca's backyard was a decent size—that part of the city had big lots—yet held nothing but yellowing grass and a few scraggly sticks that might have been decent bushes if someone had watered them.

"I know, I know," he said. "The backyard is a disgrace. But nobody sees it but me."

"It's not a disgrace," she said. "More of a wasted opportunity."

"Maybe it won't be wasted forever." He handed her a helmet. "Let's roll while there's plenty of sunset. There's a special lookout spot I want to show you."

She pulled on her helmet, hopped on behind him, and held on tight as they rolled along the weed-strewn cobblestones next to the house and then out onto the street.

The sky was gold and pink, making the precious minutes even more beautiful.

They rode out of the neighborhood and then along a park. She could tell Luca knew the route well. They turned into a part of town she'd never seen before and took a winding road that curved and bent like a meandering river.

Tina marveled at how instinctive it was to lean first one way and then the other, keeping her body in line with Luca's and the bike. The movement itself was pleasurable, like floating in a canoe on gentle waters, or coasting a bicycle down a hill.

They parked, watched the sun set, and then, when the insects came out, they pulled on their helmets again.

The single headlight sliced a path through the darkness, leading them home again.

Chapter 20

Graffiti.

Tina Gardenia arrived at the flower shop on Monday morning. She hadn't even opened the door, and her week was off to a bumpy start.

Over the weekend, someone's rotten kid had tagged the front of the shop with lime-green spray paint.

With a few curse words, Tina opened the store and headed to the back room for the supplies. She had two choices: spend several hours trying to remove the paint with chemicals, or spend ten minutes painting over it. She grabbed the paint.

Out front again, she gave the paint a quick stir then got to work with a brush. People walking by found this fascinating. She wasn't sure why seeing a woman applying paint to bricks was so much more interesting than seeing the same woman sweeping the sidewalk and setting up a flower display, but it was.

Folks kept stopping to say hello and ask what she was doing. Tina felt it was rather obvious what she was doing, but she had many friends in the area, and so she patiently explained the situation to each of them.

The ten-minute job would take at least an hour, at the rate she was going.

She was finally nearly done when Mr. Jackson, the owner of the pub, stopped by to chat. He was not Tina's favorite. Mr. Jackson was just old enough to think he knew everything, but young enough to try to flirt with her. She quickly took stock of her outfit, checking to make sure she didn't have any visible gaps for Mr. Jackson to look down.

"You'd better stock up on paint, Tina," he said. "Things are sliding downhill around here, and they're liable to get worse. I'm getting a new safe put in, for the cash. It'll be on a timelock. And I'm getting metal bars on the back door."

Was he joking? She looked up from her work.

By the look on his face, Mr. Jackson wasn't joking around.

"Why all the security?" Tina asked. "Has there been some crime wave I don't know about?"

He pointed to the graffiti with the toe of his black loafer.

"This is just the beginning," he said. "Trust me."

She returned to dabbing fresh paint over the graffiti.

"We get tagged once a year," she said. "I wouldn't worry about it."

He let out a ho-ho-ho type of laugh. "Oh, I'm sure you'll be under protection," he said, his voice ominous. "You and *your* shop."

She set down the paint brush and gave him what he wanted, her full attention.

"What are you talking about? I might be out of touch with all the local gossip since my mom's out of town. Why don't you explain it to me?"

Mr. Jackson raised his eyebrows higher and higher. "Well, you'll be protected because you're running around with the *biker*, obviously."

"What biker? Luca Lowell? He rides a bike, sure, but what does that have to do with anything? Have you been sending emails to my mother?"

He didn't answer her question. He gave her a knowing look and said, "You should be careful."

"About what? Luca bought Ralph's Garage so he could fix bikes. He's not running a crime ring."

"The whole bike thing is just a cover. That's what I heard."

"Mr. Jackson, once you see the beautiful renovation he's doing, you'll be ashamed of yourself for spreading rumors about him."

Her final words were drowned out by the sound of a motorcycle driving past them on the street.

Mr. Jackson glared down the street after the bike. "See, that's what I'm talking about. This street's going downhill. We never used to get those noisy bikes up and down this street."

"That's not new. We've always had—"

He cut her off. "And now it's all day long. Do you know some of them modify the mufflers so they're even louder? Those people like nothing more than disturbing nice folks trying to have a relaxing beer on the patio."

"We've always had bikes along this street. You've got bike parking in front of your pub. I'm sure a couple more won't be a big deal. It might be good for your business."

Mr. Jackson snorted. "You should be careful who you associate yourself with," he said.

"Is that a threat?" She turned and looked at the graffiti. It was a really large tag, covering half the width of the storefront. "Mr. Jackson, do you know anything about who spray-painted this? Is it some sort of warning, because I'm dating Luca?"

He huffed and shuffled his feet. "I don't like to get involved in politics." He stuffed his hands in his pockets and walked away quickly.

Tina finished painting over the tag. It had been years since she'd painted that section of wall, and the new paint was brighter. She'd have to get the roller and do the entire front, or at least the lower half.

Two ladies with strollers walked by, slowing to whisper to each other, eyeballing Tina the whole time. They didn't stop to ask what she was doing.

Tina quickly tidied up and retreated inside.

When she opened the register to double-check the float, her hand was shaking.

Why did Monday have to come along and ruin everything? She'd had such a nice weekend, spending most of it with Luca.

Her weekend had been perfect, and her life had seemed idyllic. No arrested development. Just a nice, completely appropriate life for a twenty-nine-year-old in the city.

Now it was Monday, and the cracks were showing.

Chapter 21

Tina didn't see Luca for a few days. He'd been busy getting the garage ready to reopen on the weekend.

He did sneak away to see her on Thursday night. He came by her place and missed bumping into Rory by about ten minutes.

Rory had been there doing another great catering job for the couple. The meal wasn't as elaborate as the first one, but in some ways that made it better. Luca said that if meatloaf and mashed potatoes and green beans hadn't been his favorite before, it certainly was now.

Over dinner, Luca talked about the problems with his contractors. Tina kept up with him, even the stuff about the itemized breakdowns of budgets, and which subtrade went over on what. Tina understood cash flow and budgets because of her work at the flower shop, but keeping up with Luca was a challenge. He would abruptly switch from one story straight into another, suddenly talking about a different guy entirely.

Tina smiled and played along, asking questions to let him know he was being heard. "Was Tim the plumber who put the drains in crooked?"

"You can't put drains in crooked. They're circular. You can't make a circle crooked. Tim is the electrician who put in the switch plate covers crooked."

"Too bad switch plate covers aren't circular," she said.

He chortled as he took another big bite of meatloaf, then struggled to keep it in his mouth. After swallowing, he said, "Good one, Flower Shop Girl. Don't hit me with one of your jokes while I'm taking a drink." He picked up the glass of sparkling water and watched her carefully as he took a sip.

Tina didn't want to hear much more about Tim and the Case of the Crooked Switch Plate Covers. She took the opportunity to ask him about more personal stuff. Not the sad details of life after his mother died when he was five, but tales about what it was like to grow up with his dad and uncle. She imagined that a home with only men would have been very different from her own upbringing. Almost the exact opposite.

Tina scooped more food onto her hungry guy's plate and asked, "Did your father keep motorbikes in the house?"

"He sure did, when he ran out of room in the garage." Luca looked off into the distance—which wasn't very far, since they were inside Tina's small cottage.

"That must have been fun," she said. "A house with three guys and no rules."

"There were some rules," he said. "Not many."

"I'd love to hear more about it."

"After things settle down with the garage, I'll take you out to the farm to meet my dad. I should probably warn you, though, he's eccentric."

"If he's anything like you, I'm sure we'll get along fine."

Luca smiled. "And what about your father? He's out of the picture?"

"*Long* gone out of the picture."

"I'm sorry to hear that."

"Oh, he's not dead," she said. "We see each other a few times a year, when he's in town." She wrinkled her nose. "He's always trying to talk me into going back to school, or doing something different with my life. He means well, but he doesn't know me."

"I'm sure he knows you better than you think he does."

There was something in Luca's tone that put her on edge.

"No," she said. "He doesn't know me. Just because your dad is some sort of macho hero that you idolize, that doesn't mean all dads are like that."

"I never said that." He set his fork down. "I didn't say that at all."

Tina got up quickly, banging the chair against the nearby kitchen counter. Why was there no space? Everything was up against everything else. Was the house getting smaller by the day?

Luca watched her. He'd taken notice that something was happening. She knew because he'd stopped eating, and there was still food on his plate.

He looked at her and asked, "What's up, Flower Shop Girl?"

"Stop calling me that! I'm not a girl. I'm almost thirty."

He ducked his head, swallowed, then said, "Okay. Noted. My cute nickname has officially worn out its welcome."

"Luca, I may not be a world traveler and adventurer like you, or someone who goes around real estate agents to make deals on a business, or argues with about a hundred contractors —seriously, is there any contractor in this entire city that you're satisfied with?—but I'll tell you one thing. I know who I am." She patted her chest. "And I know when other people *don't* know who I am."

He leaned back in his chair and looked around slowly, his gaze settling on the framed photos over the mantel.

"And who are you, Tina? All those photos are a decade old. And you still won't tell me about that prom picture."

She crossed her arms. "My pictures are old because people don't get photos printed anymore. It's all digital."

He waved one big hand dismissively. "All that digital stuff is a waste of time."

"Well, good for you, that you're too good for it. We can't all be big, burly know-it-alls with a bunch of money and their own houses and garages, now can we?"

He winced then clenched his jaw. "I earned that money. Nobody handed me anything. As for the house, you should have seen the place when I moved in. I never had anything easy. I moved away from home when I was eighteen."

She kept her arms crossed. "Good for you. When I was eighteen, I held the love of my life while he died in front of me."

A flash of expression passed over Luca's face before it went blank. He looked away.

Gruffly, he said, "I'm sorry."

That was when Tina realized he didn't know about her past. She'd assumed that he knew, thanks to Megan and her big blabbermouth. She'd hoped that he knew, so that she wouldn't have to tell him. Especially not like that.

She was too wound up to stop now. She was backed up, hemmed in by her own little house, pinned in place by her own tiny kitchen, so she kept fighting.

"If you think I don't appreciate the gift of my life, you're wrong," she said. "I feel it every day. This gift. This burden. I'm alive, and he isn't, and it's not fair. He was a better person than me, in every way. He gave everything.”

Her jaw ached like it was broken.

Luca was quiet, looking away.

Tina’s body shook and then trembled, and then that was it. No sobs. She felt herself go limp.

Tina hated to say his name, but it was the next word that came out of her mouth, and it brought the rest. “Jonathan was a good person. He never held anything back, and no matter how bad things got, he always said it was what he wanted. He always said he wouldn’t change a thing.”

Luca turned his face toward the mantel, toward the shrine of decade-old photos. His voice soft and low, he said simply, “His name was Jonathan.” He took a breath. “I’m sorry for your loss.”

“Well, you should be,” she said. Then, realizing that made no sense, said, “Thanks. It was a long time ago. I’m over it.”

Luca should have kept his mouth shut, and he did. He also should have kept a poker face, but he didn’t.

Luca lifted one eyebrow in a gesture of *oh-really?*

It pushed her over the edge.

“You should go,” she said, her voice thin and cold.

“We’re not going to talk about this?”

“There’s nothing to talk about. I hope your opening goes well on Saturday. Don’t worry about me making a scene, because I won’t be coming.”

“You won’t come to my grand opening?”

She turned her back to him. “Honestly, I don’t see the point. Just go.”

She heard the sound of his chair being pushed back. “I don’t like seeing this side of you,” he said.

If only he’d used different words to express what he meant, which was that he didn’t like seeing her upset. But he didn't have any help with his composition, and he couldn't have known that what Tina heard that night in the cabin was *I don't like you*.

She said, "Me neither, but I don't have a choice."

"You're shutting me out."

"Just go."

She heard him moving around, pulling on his boots and getting his leather jacket from the closet.

Without a word, he opened the front door, stepped out, and gently closed it again. He couldn't have known it, but she heard him sigh, because the windows were open.

After she was sure he was gone, Tina locked the door, closed all the windows and blinds, and opened the coat closet. She pushed out the shoes and settled onto the floor, her legs folded up in front of her. She pulled the door shut behind her and buried her face between the jackets.

Safe at last in the smallest of spaces, Tina Gardenia completely disappeared.

Chapter 22

Ralph's Garage had its grand re-opening on Saturday. Tina did not attend.

For the occasion, Gardenia Flowers sent over a tasteful arrangement. Tina considered signing her name on the card, or writing a personal note, but didn't.

She wrote, in block letters: *Best wishes from Gardenia Flowers.*

As far as Tina knew, the opening went well. The only motorbike "gang" to show up was a group of senior citizens who toured on road bikes together.

A month passed. Folks on the street were still concerned about the neighborhood changing, and biker gangs rolling in.

A second month passed. Folks on the street raved about how amazing Luca Lowell was, and how he had his best mechanic give their car a tuneup, and it had never run better.

A third month passed. Folks weren't talking about Ralph's Garage or Luca Lowell anymore. Mostly they were up in arms about the kid selling ice cream from his car without a license.

It was a typical summer on Baker Street.

Fall was around the corner.

Tina's sister, Megan, provided all the updates about what was going on at the garage. Megan bumped into Luca from time to time on Baker Street. Unlike Tina, she hadn't switched her route to always detour through the alley to avoid him. Unlike Tina, she hadn't quit visiting the local restaurants and getting her tea from Delilah's.

Megan reported that there was a petite woman with dark hair who dropped by the garage regularly. Luca had apparently moved on with his life.

Luca and Tina hadn't spoken to each other since the night he left her place.

That had been three months ago.

Three long months ago.

Sometimes Tina was sad their fling hadn't lasted a little longer. Other times, she was relieved, because he hadn't left too big a hole in her soul, and the wound that was there felt like it might close up any day.

Another positive thing about the whole Luca debacle was that it helped Tina get through the prom season with very few tears shed.

There'd been a day, between date five and date six, that a teenage boy had come in asking for blue flowers, to match his date's dress. Tina had laughed and talked the poor kid's ear off for an hour, telling him about her own prom, and how Jonathan had bought her a blue rose from another flower shop so he could surprise her. She told the kid about her pale-blue dress, and how everyone thought she looked like a bride. She also told him how her friends all got drunk in the bathroom, but that she was wise, and wouldn't drink their smuggled booze.

She *had* drunk the booze, as much as any of them, but changed that detail because she was trying to be a good role model. The alcohol had been someone's family's moonshine, which had been brewed in a bathtub from who knows what. Two of Tina's friends —a couple who were now married with a baby on the way—threw up all over the dance floor. Everyone ran outside because of the smell.

The janitors had gone home for the night, so the DJ pointed the speakers at the open gym doors, and everyone danced the last songs of the night outside, under the stars.

It wasn't until telling the kid with the corsage order about the good things that had happened that night that Tina had been able to fully and completely remember everything.

She'd almost forgotten about those last songs, those last dances under the stars, her head swimming from the disgusting moonshine.

Tina suspected that time was tricky, and nonlinear, like a road map that was folded like a paper fan. Thanks to the folds, two cities that were miles apart in reality could come together and touch. When it came to memories, anniversaries were those points on the map that folded back and touched each other. Sometimes the folding of time made things jumbled, so it felt like everything on the tops of the fold lines was happening at once, but really there was so much space in between everything if you let it stretch out.

That day in the flower shop, between dates five and six, the road map of Tina's life was folded a different way, collapsing in between an entirely different set of points. And wasn't that wonderful?

The boy she was talking to wasn't sure why she was even talking to him, let alone about the philosophy of time, but he was polite, and he let her talk. Folks in the neighborhood were nice to each other like that.

When the boy left, Tina realized she'd been smiling the whole time. Smiling so much her face hurt.

That particular day, at that particular time, Tina Gardenia's collected memories of her first love contained more joy than pain. It was as though time had bleached out all the sorrow, the way that a bright golden sun fades the blue dye in a rose.

Chapter 23

Megan Gardenia leaned over her sister, putting the finishing touches on Tina's hair.

It was August now, and Tina hardly ever thought about Luca. But she also hadn't been on any other dates.

Tonight was the annual Baker Street block party. Folks barricaded the street at either end of a five-block span, and people from all over the city would come to enjoy a party that went until midnight.

Lots of people dressed up for the party in summer-themed costumes, or at least got their faces painted—adults alongside kids.

Megan and Tina had been going as "flower girls" every year, and tonight was no exception. Megan had already braided her hair and twisted the braids around her head in a crown, and she did the same for Tina. The sisters had moved on to decorating their crowns, adding more fresh-cut flowers than most people would think was reasonable.

"It's getting heavy," Tina said, complaining.

"Shut up. We can get a few more flowers on your head," Megan said.

They were in the flower shop, and Rory was sitting nearby, reading gossip magazines that were several months old.

Without even looking up from the magazine, Rory said, "You two look perfect. Let's go eat."

Rory had put flowers in her hair, a few daisies stuffed into a bun. She would have never let either of the sisters touch her hair, much less braid it into a crown and stuff in an unreasonable number of flowers.

The sisters finished with their flower crowns and locked up the store, and all three young women walked out into the crowd on the street.

They shopped for beaded jewelry and tie-dyed clothing at the usual assortment of street vendors that appeared at all open-air festivals. They sampled the many delicious deep-fried foods, including a battered, deep-fried Mars bar.

A few hours in, Rory announced she was tired and anxious about people jostling her in the dark. She went home not long after sunset.

The Gardenia sisters made their way over to the band stage, where they staked out a prime spot for their blanket.

They'd just gotten comfortable when a familiar figure tossed a gray wool blanket next to theirs and took a seat.

It was Luca Lowell, and whether he knew it or not, he was sitting mere feet away from Tina. The sun had set, and his features were only lit by the street lamps, but every cell in Tina's body knew it was him.

She'd recently stopped hiding in the alley and had ventured back onto the street again, so she had glimpsed Luca around lately, but Tina always turned and went in the opposite direction to avoid him. This was different. They were seated on blankets. He could reach out and touch her, if he wanted to.

Tina turned to Megan, keeping her back to the interloper, and whispered, "Meenie. Don't look now, but you-know-who is behind me. Move slowly. Roll up the blanket, and let's go."

"Just talk to him," Megan said with a weary sigh, her voice at regular volume. "You can't avoid Luca forever."

Tina shushed Megan—not that it would do any good.

"Grow up," Megan said, then, "I love you." Megan could be blunt, but she did care.

Tina heard Luca say, "Is that Teenie and Meenie under all those flowers?"

Tina slowly turned around, a fake smile hardening on her face.

"Hi, Luca. It's us under all these flowers."

One look into his beautiful eyes, and her breath was taken away. He had become more radiant, more golden, more curly around the hair.

"That really is you," Luca said. "Nice flowers. Hey, Megan. Nice crown. You look… cute."

Megan laughed. "Good one, Lukester. Yeah, I look *real* cute, huh? I'm a flower girl. Get it?"

"I get it," he said, then he stretched out his long, denim-clad legs in front of himself on his gray blanket.

Tina gave herself a pep talk about how well she'd been doing. And then a stern lecture about not swooning over Luca if he tried anything. She didn't need him. She was better off without him. He was too big for her life, anyway. He didn't fit.

Megan said to Luca, "Hey, dude. Did you try the deep-fried Mars bar?"

"You're joking, right? That's not a real thing, is it?"

"Oh, it's real," Megan replied. "I had to share mine with Teenie because she's too delicate to order a whole one. Hey man, I've got an idea. The concert hasn't started yet, so how about I go get another deep-fried Mars bar, and you can eat half of it?"

He said, "What if I want a whole one, and I don't like sharing?"

Megan got to her feet, using Tina's shoulder to steady herself. "That's a great idea, Luca! I'd better get two. I'll be right back." Megan squeezed her sister's shoulder. "Teenie, don't go anywhere. You have to stay here and watch the stuff."

Megan walked off, leaving Tina alone with Luca.

Tina tried not to look at Luca, but he was right there. By the look of the new beard, he might not have shaved since the last time they'd spoken. His wavy brown hair was much longer, too, showing its curl. She wondered why he'd stopped shaving and getting haircuts. Was he busy at the new garage, or had something happened to him that night, too?

He cleared his throat. After a full minute of silence, he cleared it again and said, "Tina, I don't know how to be around you."

She stared straight ahead at the empty band stage.

"Just relax," Tina said. "Stuff happens. Sometimes things don't work out, because they were wrong to begin with."

"Things were wrong to begin with? I didn't know you felt that way."

"Yeah, well, we didn't exactly talk about it."

"No. We didn't."

"Thanks for cheering me up during prom season," she said. "That part was good timing."

"That part?"

"I had fun with you, for a while. I'm actually doing a lot better now. Just so you know. I, uh, took down all those old photos. I cleared a space for some new ones. My mom sent me some postcards and some pictures of herself having a great time in Italy. Maybe when I'm older, like her, I'll go there, too. I don't know. I'm just taking life one day at a time."

"That's good to hear," he said. "I'm happy for you."

"Maybe I'll get a passport, so I'm ready to go."

"Tina." His voice was deep yet quiet.

She finally turned to Luca. His face in reality was so much different than it was in her imagination. He didn't look flat and disinterested the way he did when she argued with him in her head. He was anything but flat and disinterested.

"I never meant to make you feel bad," he said.

"You didn't."

"I think I did. I don't know how it happened, but I screwed up."

"If you want to blame yourself, then fine. But, just so you know, I don't blame you." She reached over and patted the top of his shin. Channeling her sister, Tina said, "We're cool, man."

"I'm not," he said. "I shouldn't have gotten you those flowers, and that card. I thought it would be funny, apologizing for being a jerk. But then I was a jerk, and it wasn't funny at all."

"You weren't a jerk," she said. "You were honest. You told me the truth. I've had a lot of people in my life trying to get through to me for a long time, and you said what I needed to hear. I was stuck in the past. I was like a plant in a pot that's too small. But the thing is, some plants like being root bound. They prefer it. Some plants, you can only re-pot one size up at a time."

He started to smile. "Tina, are you saying you're a root-bound houseplant? You need to give yourself a little more credit."

"It's a stupid metaphor," she said. It was a metaphor she'd been thinking about a lot over the last three months, and it hadn't seemed stupid at all until now, saying the words out loud to Luca.

"It's a perfect metaphor," he said. "What kind of plant am I?"

Without hesitation, she said, "You're an oak tree."

"You've been thinking about this a lot."

She felt her cheeks flushing. She had been.

Just then, a woman walked up and flopped down on the blanket next to Luca. She asked him, "What did I miss?"

He turned to her and said, "The band hasn't started yet. You haven't missed a thing."

The woman had straight black hair cut in a bob. She was stunning and petite, with an adorably tiny nose and small ears.

She looked over at Tina. "Hi there. Do you think they'll keep us waiting for long?"

Tina was almost too stunned to speak. "I dunno," she said. "They have to play a set before the fireworks, so it shouldn't be too long."

The woman with the black bob leaned across Luca and offered Tina her hand. She introduced herself, but Tina's head was buzzing. She couldn't hear voices anymore, just the low rumble of movement around her. The night was full of dark shapes all around, and Tina felt the instinctive urge to seek the light, to seek cover.

Tina managed to keep her faculties long enough to shake the woman's pretty hand and mumble her own name with all the grace of a tranquilized bear.

Tina felt something on her shoulder. Megan plunked down beside her.

"I got the last two they had." Megan handed one paper plate with a deep-fried Mars bar to Luca. She asked Tina, "Want another bite of mine?"

Tina lurched to her feet. She felt no sensation in her body. She could barely tell her feet were on the ground.

Everyone was looking at her. Megan. Luca. Luca's new girlfriend. Strangers on neighboring blankets. Everyone looked mean.

Megan gave her sister a threatening look. It was probably just a mildly annoyed or confused look, but it registered to Tina as hateful.

"Where are you going? I said you could have a bite of mine," Megan said.

Tina went with the first idea that came to her, and moved both hands to her stomach. "I don't feel so good," she said.

"Ew," Megan said. "They have a dozen porta potties, but I don't recommend them. Go use the bathroom at the store."

"No," Tina said. "I'm going home now to beat the crowd."

Luca said, "You'll miss the fireworks."

Luca's girlfriend said, "You don't want to miss the fireworks."

Tina didn't care about the fireworks. She threw herself into the gathering crowd, into the darkness, and disappeared.

Chapter 24

The morning after the street party, Tina Gardenia woke up to the sound of her phone ringing.

The call was coming from the local hospital.

Any drowsiness she'd been feeling immediately disappeared.

"Hello?"

"Don't panic," said the female voice on the line.

"Megan? Rory?"

"I'm Doreen, and I'm a nurse," the woman said. "Are you Tina Gardenia?"

"Yes." Tina held her hand over her chest to keep her heart from leaping out of her chest. "What's going on?"

"Don't worry," the nurse said. "It's not an emergency. Someone gave us your name as an emergency contact, which is why I'm calling, but it's not urgent."

"Someone? Is it Megan Gardenia? That's my sister. If it's not urgent, why are you calling me instead of her? Did she lose her phone? What happened?"

"Ma'am," the nurse said slowly, "there's no need for alarm. I'm calling because Mr. Luca Lowell gave us your name and number as his emergency contact."

Tina was surprised, and her palms were moist from her panic sweat, and her phone slipped out of her hand like a bar of soap. It landed on her pillow, next to her on the pull-out bed. She picked up the phone again.

"Sorry," Tina said. "I lost you for a minute. What were you saying?"

"Ma'am, do you have a vehicle that's not a motorbike?"

"Like a scooter?"

The nurse chuckled. "How about a car?"

"I have a car. Why?"

"When would you be able to come and pick up Mr. Luca Lowell?"

"In my car?" Tina struggled to make sense of what was happening. The nurse was patient—she'd likely been through this a thousand times—and waited. "Oh," Tina said. "Luca's there, at the hospital, and someone needs to come and pick him up in a car. And you think I should do that."

"He asked for you," the nurse said.

"He did?"

In a friendly way, the nurse said, "He sure did. I don't think he's going to leave if you don't come get him." The nurse gave the address, but Tina knew where the local hospital was.

She pulled on some clothes, grabbed her car keys, and stepped outside. It was dark. She checked the time. It was four o'clock in the morning.

It was four in the morning, and she was driving her car to the hospital to pick up Luca Lowell because he'd asked for her specifically.

When she reached the hospital parking lot, Tina realized she wasn't exactly dressed for being anywhere public, even if it was four in the morning and a non-urgent emergency. She wore thin cotton pants, the tank top she'd been sleeping in, a zippered hoodie, and no bra. At least she was wearing shoes. They were the hideous old sneakers she used for gardening, and they were caked in cut grass.

She stepped out of the car. Anyone awake at four in the morning had bigger things to worry about than Tina's dirty shoes.

She walked in and checked in at Emergency. Since the last time she'd been there, a decade ago, they'd changed the flooring and painted the walls a different color. The big mural wall was still the same giant painting of ducks flying over a lake.

A nurse, the same one who'd phoned Tina, came to bring her to Luca. Nurse Doreen kept sneaking peeks over at Tina, pressing her lips tightly, as though to keep from laughing.

They reached a door, and the nurse said, "He's a lively one."

Tina asked, "Was anyone else hurt?"

Doreen gave her a puzzled look. "What do you mean?"

"It was a motorbike accident, right?"

Doreen shook her head. "No. He was at the Baker Street block party, helping to take down the band stand, and there was an accident."

"What? He didn't crash his motorbike?"

"I'm afraid that while he was helping with the band stand, someone in a truck backed into him. No one else was hurt."

Tina stared at the door to the room. Luca was in there. He'd been backed into by a truck. He'd been hurt. She couldn't go in there and see him like that. Someone else would have to drive him home. Why hadn't he called his new girlfriend?

The nurse asked, "Don't I know you?" Her eyebrows went up. "I do know you. You were Jonathan's girl."

Tina took another look at Doreen. She was nearing retirement age. Ten years ago, her gray hair had been mostly black, so Tina hadn't recognized her at first.

"It's you," Tina said. "Sorry. With everything going on, I didn't know it was you."

The nurse said, "And I'm sorry I called you Jonathan's girl. You do have a name. It's just that I remember people through their connection to the patients.”

“Don’t apologize. I’m proud to be Jonathan’s girl. I’ll always be his girl. And he really liked you, Doreen.”

Doreen looked wistfully at the door. “You’re a lucky girl to find love twice. Now get in there and take that guy home before we decide to keep him.”

“He’s not...”

“Go,” Doreen said sternly. “If I were your age, I wouldn’t keep a man like that waiting long.”

Tina remembered Doreen had always been one of the sassier, tell-it-like-it-is nurses. That was why Jonathan had liked her so much.

Doreen opened the door and shoved Tina in.

“Teenie Weenie Beanie!” Luca was sitting up on a bed, holding his arms out for a hug. “Teenie Baneenie!” He looked okay, except for the fresh cast on his left foot. And the fact that he was clearly quite high on painkillers. That explained why he’d had Nurse Doreen contact Tina at four in the morning rather than someone more appropriate.

“It’s me,” Tina said. “They told me I have to give you a ride home.”

He gave her the kind of innocent look that only someone high on painkillers could give. “Where’d you go? You left before the band came on.”

“I wasn’t feeling well.”

He nodded gravely. “Bathroom emergency. I totally understand.” He waved one hand. “Porta potties. Nope. Nope, nope, nope. Just say no to porta potties.”

“They got you on the good stuff, huh?”

He widened his eyes, staring at her with unmistakably enlarged pupils. “I don’t do drugs,” he said. “Nope, nope, nope. Just coffee.”

He was wearing the same shirt he'd been in when she'd seen him the night before at the street party. The bottom of his jeans had been cut away on the cast side, and his bare knee was exposed.

"Luca, what happened? Did someone hit you with a truck?"

He waved one hand, paw-like. "Just a bump. Didn't even leave a scratch."

"But you broke your foot."

"Pfft," he said. "Barely."

"Is the rest of you okay? No internal injuries?"

His face lit up. "Do you want to check?"

She said nothing.

He patted himself. "I'm okay. Hey, did I say that out loud? Did I ask you to check my internal guts and stuff? I apologize. That was not cool. Not cool at all. I'm sorry I am such a jerk. If you ask me, I don't like him at all."

"You don't like who?"

"Luca," he said. "That guy's a real jerk."

"He sure is, but I'm going to give him a ride home anyway." Tina walked over to the wheelchair and unfolded it. Time folded up like a road map. A sense memory of unfolding wheelchairs came back to her then quickly receded to where it had been.

Luca, who'd stopped babbling, eased himself off the bed, onto the wheelchair, and grabbed the pair of crutches that had been resting against the wall.

"Ready to roll out," he said.

As she wheeled him out of the room, she asked, "Where's your friend?"

"You're my friend. And your sister is my friend. But you're my favorite one. We're going to get married. Did you know that?"

"You are so high right now."

He turned, craning his neck as he stared up at her. "Don't tell the nurses," he whispered.

When they reached Tina's car, they discovered the hard way that he didn't easily fit in the front seat. Tina leaned over him to adjust the seat, pushing it as far back as it would go.

Luca patted her on the butt. "I missed this butt," he said.

She pushed his hands away. "You're such a jerk."

"Boo," he said. "Hiss. We hate Luca."

Finally, they were on the road.

Luca said, "I can't go home."

"Is that where your girlfriend is? She's probably worried sick about you."

"I can't go to my house because there's too many stairs," he said. "It's too big. I need somewhere small. You have to take me to your house, Tina."

"That's not going to happen."

"I won't get out of the car if you don't take me to your teenie weenie beanie house."

"Fine, you big baby. But just until you sober up."

They got to Tina's house. The bed was still how she'd left it, unfolded.

Luca dropped the crutches and fell onto the bed like it was his own. Within seconds, he was fast asleep, still in his clothes. He wore one big boot, on the foot that wasn't in a cast. She pried it off his foot for him. He stirred but didn't wake up. He sleepily rolled to the side of the bed—it was a king-sized mattress, which was why the couch was so large— leaving plenty of room beside him.

Tina yawned. It wasn't quite five o'clock yet.

She kicked off her gardening sneakers, pulled a spare blanket from the hall closet, and lay down next to Luca.

She didn't think she'd be able to sleep, but she did.

Chapter 25

Tina woke up to the sound of cursing nearby.

Luca was in her kitchen. By the smell of it, he was burning toast. By the sound of it, he was knocking stuff over like a bull in a china shop. There was barely enough space in the kitchen area for him, but certainly not for him and his crutches.

"Good morning, sleepyhead," Luca said. He leaned back on the counter and stuffed burned toast into his mouth. "I hope you don't mind me rustling up some food. I need to eat something with my painkillers, or I might get funny."

"Funny like you were last night?"

"Last night's a blur. You'll have to catch me up."

Tina rolled off the bed and started folding it back into a sofa.

Luca said, "Don't do that. I was going to bring you breakfast in bed."

"I don't like crumbs in my bed," she said. "Or people who don't pay rent here."

"You want rent?" He smiled as he finished the toast. "How much?"

She ignored his question as she tossed the couch cushions back in place. "If you were hungry, you should have woken me up. You should be sitting. Your foot should be elevated, so it doesn't swell up inside your cast."

"Tina, it's just a cast. I can make toast."

She went to the kitchen, grabbed his big arm, and tried to pull him out. He leaned back and wouldn't budge.

"Get out of here," she said. "You're banging into everything with your crutches."

"I'm not going," he said.

"Go sit on the couch. I'll make you some eggs."

"Nope," he said. "I might be a jerk, and I might make mistakes, but I don't make the same one twice." She was still pulling on his arm when he let go of the counter. He fell against her, wrapping his arms around her. "Oops," he said. "Clumsy me."

"What are you doing?" Her voice was muffled from having his shoulder against her mouth.

She felt the rumble of his voice in his chest as he spoke. "You're not pulling me or pushing me out of your life again. I shouldn't have left you that night."

"I want you to go."

"If you really want me to go, I will, but I don't think you do. Look at yourself. You're hugging me."

"If I let you go, you'll fall down and break everything in my kitchen. Again."

She squeezed her eyes shut and tensed her body, rejecting his hug while still being in it.

"When did I break everything in your kitchen?"

She didn't answer.

"You mean I broke your heart when I left," he said.

"You did."

"What about you? You didn't come to my grand opening. You sent me those boring funeral flowers and a generic card. You might as well have stuck an ice pick in my chest."

"That was different."

"You broke my heart," he said. "I barely made it through the night. I've been barely making it through a lot of nights."

Tina relaxed into the hug. There was a lump in her throat. She managed to choke out, "I don't understand what happened with us."

He reached up and stroked her upper back. "We had our first fight," he said. "That's what happened. And I didn't know how to apologize. My bookkeeper quit helping me with my text messages, and I couldn't go see my favorite florist for advice."

She pulled away and poked him in the stomach with two fingers. "Don't make jokes, Luca. Don't make me laugh."

"I shouldn't have left you here that night," he said, gazing down into her eyes. "But I was stubborn, and I thought I was right and you were wrong. Or maybe I was scared."

"Why would you be scared?"

"My wrist hurts." He kept looking into her eyes. "I know I only broke my foot last night, but when I fell, I reached out to break my fall. I've been thinking about this all morning, and the same thing must have happened with us."

"Are you saying I hurt your wrist?"

"Yes and no. I think I realized I was falling, and I freaked out. I tried to stop my fall, but I only made it worse." He leaned down and gently kissed her. "I tried to stop my fall, but then I broke both of us."

She pulled away, slipped out of his arms, and took three steps back, until she was against the back of the sofa, with nowhere to go.

Luca said, "Don't you dare run. I've got crutches, and I'm not afraid to use them."

"Where would I go?"

He grinned. "I knew there was a reason I loved this house."

She looked away. "Luca, don't kiss me, and don't look at me like that. You have a girlfriend. She seemed nice."

"I do? Can you tell me who it is, because I don't know."

"Very funny. The woman you were with at the street party last night."

He wrinkled his nose. "Her? You know all about her. She's the one I sent the other apology flowers to." He shook his head. "Tina, she's not my girlfriend. She's married."

"You fool around with married ladies? You're not just a jerk. You're disgusting."

"It's not like that," he growled, sounding annoyed.

"You kept telling me you were a jerk, so I shouldn't be surprised." Tina rounded the sofa, edging toward the door.

Luca grabbed his crutches and hobbled toward her. "Wait a minute. When you came to my house for dinner, you met Chris and his wife. Why would you think she was my girlfriend?"

"You're sleeping with your neighbor's wife? That's low."

"No, Tina. I'm not sleeping with anyone, except you, last night. You are so exasperating!"

"At least I don't sleep with my neighbor's wife!"

"Slow down. I sent apology flowers to my neighbor's wife because she tried to set me up on a blind date with a friend. Then I was a jerk because I spent the whole date talking about another girl."

Tina edged toward the door, saying nothing.

Luca said, "I wouldn't stop talking about the pretty girl I met at the flower shop. I couldn't get her out of my head. And that's what the second bouquet was all about." He hobbled one step closer, awkwardly navigating the tight space on his crutches.

Tina reached for the door handle but didn't turn it. "You're not seeing anyone else now, and you weren't then?"

"Not since Jessica Fitzgibbon, which I think we can all agree was a giant mistake."

What Luca was trying to say to Tina finally sank in.

"Oh," she said, twisting the door handle. The door cracked, letting a breeze into the tiny space.

"Tina Gardenia, if you open that door and run out of here, I *will* chase you down on these crutches, and it won't be pretty."

"You should be resting," she said. "You need to put your foot up."

"I would happily rest, if I could get the prettiest, sweetest, funniest woman I've ever met to stop hating me."

"I don't hate you," she said.

He pointed to his lips. "Prove it."

Chapter 26

It was time for dinner, and Luca was still in Tina's house, still wearing the cut-apart jeans he'd worn there from the hospital.

He was sitting on the sofa with his foot propped up while Tina prepared a meal using the new cookbook she'd gotten from Rory the week before. Over the last three months, Tina hadn't just thrown out a bunch of things from high school. She'd also been learning some new skills, such as how to make food that wasn't nachos.

"I'll have to throw these jeans away and get new ones," Luca said. "Unless you want these to make a pair of cut-offs?"

"Your jeans would be way too big on me," she said, not looking up from the bowl of ingredients she was mixing.

"But there's something in them for you."

She chuckled. "I bet there is."

"Naughty girl," he said. "I mean there's something in the pocket for you. Do you want it?"

She walked over to him and held out her hand. "Sure. Whatever."

He placed a tiny charm in the palm of her hand. A heart.

"It's all yours now," he said. "Even if you drop it, and step on it, and bend it out of shape, it's still yours. I don't want it back."

"You had this in your pocket?"

"I've had it in my pocket every day for the last three months. Except one day when I thought I lost it in the washing machine, but then I found it in the filter. Don't worry. It's clean."

She stared at the heart and thought about all the times she'd taken the alley to work, or ducked into a store to avoid seeing Luca on the street. All the times she'd missed her chance to get Luca's heart back.

"I can understand if you don't want my stupid heart," he said. "If I were you, I wouldn't take me back either, because I'm not always a fan of Luca Lowell. He doesn't always do the right thing."

"Don't say that."

"It's true. If I hadn't gotten backed into by a truck last night and hadn't gone to the hospital, I don't know if you ever would have brought me back to your house. Back into your life."

"My tiny house, and my tiny life."

He shrugged. "It's big enough for me." He stretched out on the sectional. "You'll have a hard time kicking me out again."

"Luca, I can't make you any promises."

"Yes, you can. You can promise to give me a second chance the next time I screw up."

"You didn't screw up. I did. I'm the one who kicked you out."

"Then I'll give you a second chance. I won't be a chicken and take the alley to work so I don't run into you."

"You did that?"

"Only for about a week, until your sister busted me sneaking through the alley like a burglar, and tore me a new one." He rubbed his beard. "You know, now that I'm thinking over my conversations with her, it's all making sense. She must have thought Chris's wife was my girlfriend. The two of them stop by the garage a lot, but not always together. I thought your sister was being—well, you know how she is— but now I think I understand what was *really* going on."

Tina looked down at the heart in her palm then at Luca. She closed her fingers around the charm.

"Don't worry," she said. "I'm not going to drop it again."

There was a scratch at the door. Luca rolled himself along the couch, reached out with one long arm, and opened the door.

Muffins strolled in like he owned the place.

Luca exclaimed, "Kitty!"

Muffins jumped up on the couch and started sniffing Luca's cast. Then he meowed about dinner.

Luca picked the cat up gently and held him like a baby. "You are a cutie patootie," he said, then he cleared his throat and said gruffly, "Yes, uh. This is a healthy cat specimen. A strong hunter. I can tell by his, uh, ample midsection."

Tina said, "That's some pretty impressive baby talk for a big, tough guy like you."

"Big, tough guys have feelings, too," Luca said. "And they like cats."

Chapter 27

Tina Gardenia was as happy as a cat with a full belly.

She had kept Luca Lowell's heart safely on her charm bracelet, and it had been wonderful.

It was Sunday morning again, and Luca was clunking around in the tiny kitchen on one bare foot and one walking cast, making coffee by the smell of it.

Tina snuggled Muffins close to her face. "You're a handsome boy," she cooed.

"I know you're talking to the cat," Luca said. "Why don't you talk to me like that?"

"You already get more than enough compliments, Mr. Lowell."

"How many dunks do I dunk your tea bags?"

"You don't dunk. Just pour the water on and let it steep."

"How's it going to steep if you're not dunking?"

"Fine," she said. "Give it... seven dunks."

"Gotcha. Seven dunks." He started counting them out.

Tina nuzzled the ginger cat sprawled out on the couch. "You're the prettiest boy in the world," she said.

Luca growled, "I heard that."

"Focus on your dunking."

"Darn it. I lost count."

"That'll teach you for listening in on other people's private conversations."

Luca snorted and went back to dunking.

For the last two weeks, Muffins had been coming to visit at the tiny house regularly, and Luca had been pretending to be a jealous boyfriend. He and the cat were bonding on their own, though, often snuggling up on the couch together, watching their favorite shows. Luca liked true crime shows, and Muffins liked a warm lap and chin scratches.

Tina buried her face in Muffins's belly and inhaled. The cat always smelled so good. Tina's attention became overwhelming, and Muffins got up and flicked his tail in annoyance.

"Why do you keep sneaking over here?" Tina asked the cat.

He flicked his tail.

"Oh, Meenie's not giving you enough attention, is she?"

Luca brought Tina her tea, moving with surprising agility for a guy in a cast. "Careful, it's hot," he said.

"You take such good care of me."

"Hah!" He hopped back to the kitchen to watch the coffee maker finish brewing his cup. "You're the one who looks after me," he said. "Trust me on this one. For a guy who grew up with just his father, I notice when a woman is being good to me."

"Who wouldn't be good to you? You're adorable."

He snorted, which only makes him look more adorable.

"You'd be surprised," he said. "I don't like to talk about the past, because it's all in the past, but I've dated a few women with funny ideas about how things should be."

"Like Jessica Fitzgibbon? Somehow, I can't imagine you putting up with a woman like that for long."

The coffee maker finished, and he hopped over to the couch to sit next to Tina.

"Cheers." He clinked his mug against her tea cup. "What's going on? You're quiet this morning."

"I'm worried about my sister."

"Meenie? Why would you worry about her?"

Muffins climbed onto Luca and took possession of his lap. Luca patted the cat with his big hands, stroking him hard enough to pull Muffins's upper eyelids back so he looked like he was in a wind tunnel. The cat loved it, preferring Luca's lap over Tina's. The little traitor.

"She's been acting weird lately. That's why the Muff-meister is always over here."

"Your sister's fine. The cat is obviously in love with me."

Tina rolled her eyes, even though it was true. "I'm worried that her loser self-help group is becoming her main relationship. Do you think it might be a cult?"

"If she shaves her head and takes an interest in the tambourine, then we'll get involved." He leaned over and planted a kiss on Tina's lips. She didn't like the taste of coffee, except for on Luca's mouth. She could taste that all day.

"Meenie's always had trouble with relationships."

He sipped his coffee, listening without commenting.

"When we were eight, she'd hold boys down and kiss them," Tina said. "One family moved away from the neighborhood because she was allegedly bullying their son."

"Was she?"

"By today's standards, probably. But it didn't seem that bad at the time. We were all just kids. Kids do stuff like that."

"I would have loved to have gotten bullied like that," Luca said. "By a girl, of course." He wrinkled his nose. "But not your sister, of course."

"You wouldn't have been her type," Tina said. "You don't back down."

"Megan's got a good heart," Luca said. "And she cares about other people. You know, I've got a mechanic at the shop who might be her type."

Tina patted Luca's chest. "You're the one with the good heart." She kept rubbing, enjoying the ridges of his muscles under his shirt. He grabbed her hand and kissed her fingertips.

Luca asked huskily, "Is it too early for a game of Scrabble?"

It wasn't too early at all.

Chapter 28

Tina and Luca were playing Scrabble late Tuesday night when there was a knock at the door.

Luca said, "Is that Rory, back again?"

"You wish," Tina said. "You like having her on your side so you guys can gang up on me."

Since they'd been introduced to each other, her best friend and her boyfriend had gotten along well. Quite well, considering Rory's quirks. Luca respected Rory's boundaries and her cooking. Rory appreciated Luca's patience, and his relaxed energy seemed to be helping her open up. She'd even joked about him getting a job as a sort of therapy pet for anxious people like her.

Tina answered the door. It wasn't Rory after all.

It was Megan Gardenia, who'd had to knock because Tina had been keeping the door locked lately.

Megan peered around Tina's shoulders. "Did I interrupt anything spicy? It looked like the cottage was shaking on the foundations again. We might need to have another seismic assessment done, if we keep having all these localized earthquakes."

Tina resisted the urge to strangle her sister. "Meenie, do you have to be so rude, all the time?"

Luca called out, "Hey, Meenie! We've got an open bottle of wine. Come in and help yourself."

Megan bulged her eyes at her sister. "At least *some* people know how to make a girl feel welcome."

She came in and tossed aside her light jacket. She was wearing her rudest T-shirt. It was a souvenir someone brought her from Beijing. The city's name was abbreviated to a B and a J, so it read I-HEART-BJ.

And the girl wondered why she didn't have a boyfriend. Where to start?

Meenie looked over the pile of Luca's stuff on the dining table. "You guys could trade me for the big house for a while, if you want."

Luca and Tina assured her they were just fine in the cottage. Megan helped herself to the open wine and joined the couple in their Scrabble game on the coffee table. They only had one word down on the board, which Luca cleared quickly. The truth was, they hadn't been playing Scrabble when Megan had knocked on the door, but they'd never admit it.

Luca had finally read Meenie's crude T-shirt and was having a hard time keeping a straight face. Tina would have apologized for her sister barging in, but he seemed happy enough. Luca hadn't grown up with any siblings, let alone sisters, so this was still a novelty for him. She was glad he liked it, because Tina could imagine all of them having holidays together, and it was a nice picture in her head.

Luca wrestled the wine bottle from Megan to refill his own glass. "Your sister was telling me you're in a club Tuesday nights," he said. "I hope it's not the kind where you sign over all your personal possessions."

She gave him the same stink-eye look she used to give other wrestlers in high school, before she knocked them to the ground—sometimes in the cafeteria.

"It's a group for people who have problems," Megan said tersely. "Not that I have problems myself. I thought it was a weight loss group, but now I still go because it's fun."

"That's nice of you," Luca said. "Your self-help group sounds interesting. Tina told me about it. I hope you don't mind."

"It's not a secret, you big dummy," Megan said.

Tina kicked Megan in the shin. "Behave yourself."

"I'm sorry," Megan said to Luca.

Tina asked, "What's gotten into you tonight?"

"There's a new guy at group," Megan told them, and gave the rundown about a guy named Drew, and their strange situation. She had a sweet smile on her face the whole time.

Tina hadn't seen that kind of smile on Meenie's face in a long time.

Megan let out a girly sigh, staring dreamily into outer space. "No offense, Luca, but he's really hot. Way hotter than you."

Luca was hanging on her every word. "Why would I take offense to that?"

Megan explained that the new guy was way hotter than Luca. She then went on to describe him, in detail. She went on for a while about his argyle socks and how they hugged his ankles. Also about how she wanted to lick his face.

Tina started to get a sinking feeling, based on the details, so she tried to make it clear that Megan should stay away.

"I disagree," Luca said, then he went on to talk about fate and destiny. He didn't know Megan's full background, so he had no idea he was throwing gas on the fire.

Tina tried to focus on her letter tiles and words, letting the other two talk. Megan had a defiant personality—some might call it a disorder—so if Tina put her foot down and officially came out against the guy, Megan would only want him more.

Neither of them were trying to play the Scrabble board strategically, so Tina beat them easily.

Megan had one of her tantrums and tossed the board on the floor "by accident."

When Megan was in the washroom, Tina whispered to Luca, "She's a sore loser. Sorry I didn't warn you about that."

"It must have been fun growing up with a sister," he said.

"You can have her."

"I will. When we get married, she'll be my sister."

Tina was stunned. Talking about marriage? Already? Luca hadn't been kidding around when he'd given her his heart to keep forever.

She nonchalantly said, "My family is all yours."

Grinning, he pulled her in for a kiss.

They were interrupted by Megan, stomping through on her way to the front door. She saw them kissing and yelled, "At least wait until I'm out of the house!"

"I love you, sis!" Tina called after her.

Megan blew them a kiss on her way out, stumbling as she did. She'd had a lot of wine, so it was a good thing she didn't have far to go to get home.

As soon as Megan was gone, Tina jumped up and closed the blinds. Then she turned off all the lights, except for the small one in the kitchen.

"Someone forgot to pay the power bill," Luca said.

"If we keep the lights low, hopefully nobody else will knock on the door."

"It's pretty dark in here. Be careful you don't trip over my cast."

Tina immediately tripped over his cast. She fell into his lap, laughing.

Chapter 29

Tina and Luca rode the motorbike into the hospital parking lot. Luca's arms were wrapped around Tina, and she was seated in front of him.

Luca had been telling her the bike was hers now, but she felt it was too early in the relationship for such extravagant gifts. They'd only been back together for a few months, just long enough for her to learn how to ride a bike, but by the way things were going, she'd probably relent and start calling it *her* bike soon. It was her favorite, a vintage model that was a bit smaller than the one they'd taken out on their first date.

The doctors didn't want Luca riding while his foot was still in the cast. They did say he could go on a few rides, but only if someone else drove. Tina was sure the suggestion was a joke on the doctor's part, but Luca had called a friend that night to set her up with lessons.

Tina liked riding. She liked the rumble of the engine and the way leaning from side to side for balance felt like her whole body was in the flow of the universe. It was great exercise, too. She might never have muscles like Luca's, but she was building strength and balance.

Plus she looked really hot in her own pair of black leather pants.

Luca hopped off the bike on his boot side and waited for her to get under his arm. The bad part about taking the bike anywhere was the lack of storage for crutches. People already stared enough as it was, with a woman in front and a guy with a big cast on his foot as passenger.

The couple hopped their way into the waiting room and took a seat.

Luca was excited about getting the cast off. He'd brought along a new pair of boots that laced up, so he didn't strain the mending bone.

Tina picked up a magazine, and Luca sighed.

She put down the magazine again and turned to him. "What's going on?"

"My foot is itchy inside the cast. Slide over here and distract me from it."

The waiting room held several people, all reading magazines, pretending they weren't listening.

"Distract yourself," she said. "Read that science magazine."

"I already read it," he said. "Back in the third grade, when it came out."

"Read it again."

One of the older ladies seated nearby giggled and gave Tina a knowing look.

"I'm bored," Luca said.

"Only boring people get bored," she said.

"Pay attention to me."

"Have you been taking lessons from Muffins about how to be annoying? What's next? Are you going to climb into my lap and rip up my magazine with your claws?"

"I know how to get your attention." He hopped off his chair and knelt on the floor in front of her. "Hello," he said.

"There's no room for you on my lap," she said.

The older lady across from them giggled again.

Luca said, "Who do you love more, me or Muffins?"

"Since you're here right now and he isn't, I'll say you."

Luca turned and explained to the giggling older lady, "If you saw the cat, you'd understand. He's a fine cat."

Luca turned back to Tina. He was still on his knees. "Tina, I have a question for you."

The sound of magazines being flipped stopped abruptly. Everyone in the waiting room was looking their way.

Tina's cheeks burned, and her pulse rushed in her ears. He was joking around, as usual, but it was close enough to feeling real that she was nervous.

With her voice high and stretched thin, Tina said, "Yes, Luca? What is it?"

He pulled from his pocket a tiny charm for her bracelet.

She leaned forward, eager to see what it was. She was wearing her charm bracelet that day, as she always did, so she was eager to add the new one. But what was it?

"That's funny," Luca said. "It looked a lot bigger in the store." He dropped the charm into her hand. It was a teeny, tiny ring. An engagement ring.

"Luca," she said.

The older lady giggled nervously.

"Hang on," Luca said. "Don't say anything yet." He reached into his pocket again, and that time he pulled out a full-sized ring. One that would fit on her finger.

It was the second most beautiful thing Tina Gardenia had ever seen.

The *most* beautiful thing she'd ever seen was Luca's blue eyes, glistening as he looked up at her and asked, "Will you marry me?"

The word came out of her mouth without even registering in her brain. "Yes."

She leaned forward and wrapped her arms around his big shoulders.

The other patients, and some nurses who'd approached quietly, clapped and cheered.

Tina knew this wasn't the way people got engaged. She'd heard all the stories from her newlywed friends. They didn't do it in a hospital waiting room, in front of a giant mural of ducks flying over a lake.

Some of the worst moments of Tina's life had happened there in that waiting room. Later, Luca would say it had been spontaneous. He'd picked up the ring the day before and planned to propose to her in a few months, or maybe in a year, but then, that day in the waiting room, he asked himself why he was waiting.

As he pushed the ring onto her finger, Tina's life folded and rearranged itself. Time was no longer linear, and every moment of her life was happening at the same time. She sensed a future, hiding just out of sight. It was a beautiful future, full of joy, just like her past. The joy had always been there, and it had taken the second love of her life to show her the way.

Or perhaps it was the third great love of her life, if you counted Muffins.

If you enjoyed this novel, you'll love Angie Pepper's other books set on Baker Street, featuring more great romantic comedy plus guest appearances by your favorite characters!

For a full list of titles, visit the author's website at
www.angelapepper.com

Thanks for reading!